BLOOD
BROTHERS

BLOOD BROTHERS

KENT CONWELL

AVALON BOOKS
NEW YORK

PRINTED IN THE UNITED STATES OF AMERICA
ON ACID-FREE PAPER
BY HADDON CRAFTSMEN, BLOOMSBURG, PENNSYLVANIA

To Susan, who has become a fine young woman
with the world at her feet.
I love you.
And to my wife, Gayle, without whom
I would have never written one word.
I love you.

Chapter One

My Apache father, Chato, was a wise man.

A Mimbre Apache, he gave me one of life's greatest gifts, the wisdom to view life with courage and a smile. I like to think I did my best to follow his teaching, but when I looked up at the young private standing at rigid attention in the open doorway, my grin froze, and a sense of dread gripped my heart with an icy hand.

He threw me a smart salute. He didn't have to say a word. I knew why he was here. For weeks, for months, for years, I had whispered secret prayers to the sun and the moon, and to the white man's god that this particular time would never come. But now, I sensed the time had arrived. The forces against which I had prayed for years were in motion, and I could do nothing to stop them.

Still—perhaps I was wrong. Perhaps the young sol-

1

dier's mission was not what I expected. "What is it, Private?"

His reply crushed my hopes. "Mr. Cook would like to see you, Mr. Moore, sir." His Adam's apple bobbed when he spoke, and his voice was squeaky and nervous. Thin, but straight as one of old Abe Lincoln's split rails, the boy couldn't have been more than sixteen. He cleared his throat and added, "Right away, sir."

John Salmon Cook and I had known each other for years. He seldom sent orderlies for me, but when he did . . .

Head spinning, my thoughts confused, I mumbled, "Thanks, Private." Numbed, I hauled my own lanky frame from the comfortable wingback chair in front of the fireplace. I stared blankly into the comforting flames a few moments longer, reluctant to leave their warmth.

Washington, D.C., in the late winter drives a chill deep into a man's bones, especially this week-long icy drizzle that had whistled in between snowstorms.

I bundled well against the weather, and as I turned my shoulder into the bone-chilling wind, I once again pulled up the dream that had driven me for the last few years, the ranch, our ranch, a small valley with good grass nestled high in the mountains of Wyoming, just the place for the two of us, my Apache brother and me. And, I thought with sadness, it would have also been a fine place for *Sons-ee-ah-ray*, had she lived.

Ten minutes later, I stood before John Cook, director of the United States Secret Service, a new governmental agency only six years old.

John Cook stared up at me, his usually smiling face now somber, his gray eyes clouded like the weather outside. He nodded to a chair. "Sit down, Ben."

I remained standing. I knew this was no sociable visit. "What is it, John?" Out of habit, I reached for the rawhide loop on my holster. My finger flipped air. I realized I was wearing no weapon.

He rose and crossed the office to the battered cherrywood credenza against the opposite wall. Without asking, he splashed Kentucky bourbon into two tumblers and handed me one.

He stared at me. His eyes bored into the deepest recesses of my mind where I had tucked away the questions I refused to ask. "You'll need it."

I read the unwanted answer to my unasked question in his eyes. "My brother?"

John Cook downed his drink in one gulp and nodded. "I'm sorry." He set the glass on his desk and picked up a handwritten message and handed it to me. "This came just minutes ago."

As I skimmed over the telegram, my heart sank. I cursed to myself as I had never cursed before. When I finished, I looked up at John Cook, who was busy studying the glass in his hand. I set my untasted glass of bourbon on the desk and reread the telegram.

I suppressed the Apache anger trying to force its way through the layers of the white man's culture I had acquired these last ten or eleven years, but I couldn't keep the resentment from my voice. "I thought our agency was concerned with counterfeiting, not Indians."

John Cook shrugged. "This is a special request."

I shook my head. Anyone who has been with the

service even two weeks knew what "special request" meant. You carried out the orders, or you quit. I held up the memo. "This doesn't mean *Nah-kay-yen* is mixed up with those renegade Apache. You know yourself," I added, half in jest, half in seriousness. "All Indians look the same to the white man."

A smile broke the older man's rugged face, a face that reminded me of the scarred bark of the Ponderosa pine. He replied in a soft growl. "I know, Ben. For your information, despite what we've heard, I don't think your brother is involved either, but *they* . . ." He made a short, upward nod of his head, indicating his superiors. "They don't listen to what I think. The Secretary of the Interior has ordered the Secret Service to look into the matter, try to discover just exactly what is happening. I figured you'd want first shot at being the one to find out what the blazes is going on out in Arizona Territory."

I eyed him skeptically. "Is that all the Secretary wants to know, just what's going on?"

My old friend pursed his lips and looked me straight in the eyes. He shook his head. "No. He named your brother specifically. He wants him brought in for questioning and probably a trial." John Cook hesitated. "I don't like saying it, son, but that's what will be expected of whoever goes to Arizona."

I studied John Salmon Cook for several long seconds. I had often wondered just what my reply would be when this question came, and now, I was surprised to realize I didn't even have to consider my response. I thought of the ranch, of my brother, of our childhood. "I can't, John. You understand. *Nah-kay-yen's* my brother. Whether Apache or white, a man doesn't turn on his brother. This country just finished a war that put brother against brother, and it was a bad thing.''

John Cook studied me, and a faint grin curled the edges of his lips. "I don't blame you, Ben. I couldn't do it either were it my brother. But we've been friends too long for me not to give you first shot at it.''

For several seconds, our eyes met in silent understanding. We had only known each other for four years, but our commitment to each other was for a lifetime. I saved his life from a handful of riverside muggers in Saint Louis back in '67, and he brought me into the service, and gave my life some purpose. John Cook was as close to a white father as I could remember. So naturally, I was disappointed that I couldn't do as he requested.

"Who're you going to send in my place?" I asked.

"Guess.''

I had figured as much. "It's a tough trip, John. And you're getting long in the tooth.''

He laughed. "Don't worry about me, sprout. I can take care of myself.''

I grinned.

In his fifty-four years, John Salmon Cook had freighted along the Erie Canal, bullwhacked from Saint Louis to Oregon, warred in Mexico with Zachary Taylor, and fought at Buena Vista with Ulysses S. Grant and Robert E. Lee. He was tough as a mesquite post, ornery as a broomtail bronc, and stubborn as a longhorn steer, but the West demanded more than just tough and hardheaded and stubborn.

I extended my hand. "Thanks, John. With you, at least I know *Nah-kay-yen* will get fair treatment.''

"That he will, Ben. That he will. Now, I need you to fill me in on some details. His name, for example. Nah-ah—.'' He grimaced. "I'll never remember the Apache name. What's his English name? You told me once, but I forgot."

"Keen Sighted."

"Keen Sighted? That's it. I knew it was a funny name of some kind. Does it mean what I think?"

"Yep." I explained. "I've never seen a man with eyes as sharp as his. When we were young, he not only could spot game that was almost invisible to the rest of us, but he could also tell us whether it was a male, female, old, young . . . you name it. And no one knows more woodcraft or understands animal habits any better than Keen Sighted."

As we spoke, we retired to John Cook's study where I spent the next few hours giving him all the information he could absorb.

That John Salmon Cook could have handled the job in his prime, I had no doubt. He had risen from the ranks of Company D, 53d Pennsylvania, to colonel in less than two years, earning several decorations for bravery, two of which came in the Union defeat at the first Bull Run on Saturday and Sunday, July 20 and 21, 1861, and a third under General McClellan in the defense of Washington, D.C., in September 1862. He was in the Seven Days fight, Antietam, first Fredericksburg, Vicksburg, Jackson, and the Wilderness. In those years, he could have handled any situation, even the West, maybe even the Apache.

But six years behind a desk dulls reflexes and perceptions, skills essential for survival in the West. That's what scared me.

ocotillo, struggled to contain several broken down nags, any of which would have been better off in the cooking pots of the Pimos.

No, Tucson had not changed. I knew no one in the little adobe village then or now. And no one knew me, and that sat just fine with me. But I was anxious to ride out to the rancheria, to pay visit to my Apache father, Chato, whose Apache name was *Kay-tanh*, and my mother, Broken Knee. We would have a joyous reunion. I just wished that *Sons-ee-ah-ray* still lived.

Sheriff Samuel Black of Tucson narrowed his eyes and wiped the tobacco juice off his scruffy beard and tugged his gun belt up over his watermelon belly and informed me that the G Troop had set up a temporary bivouac thirty miles or so to the west beyond the Tucson Mountains. The sun had dropped below the horizon by the time I emerged from the sheriff's, so I decided to indulge myself and spend the night between clean sheets on a soft bed.

Leaving my roan pony with the hostler, I checked into the hotel, enjoyed a warm bath, and dressed in my clean clothes. My traveling duds I dropped off at a Chinese laundry across the street when the obsequious little man promised to have them back in my room by midnight.

Standing in front of the hotel and enjoying the warm night breeze wrapping around me, I let my mind wander, and for a moment, as I gazed up at the Santa Catalinas looming over the small village, I was back up in the Arizona mountains again, enjoying the unfettered freedom of the wild animals and the Apache.

My stomach growled, reminding me that the only

grub I had eaten that day had been the leftover fore-
quarters of a stringy rabbit I had roasted the night
before.

I looked up and down the street for a cafe. The main
street was lit by rectangular patches of lamplight pouring from the store windows. The street reminded me
of a yellow-and-black checkerboard. Maybe half a
dozen businesses had boardwalks. The remainder just
swept off the dirt and gravel soil in front of their door.

Strolling down the dusty street, I peered into the
lighted buildings, of which saloons and cantinas
seemed to make up the majority. On the corner, I
found a small cafe with a boardwalk. The inside was
well lit with candles and a couple coal oil lanterns.
The building had a wooden floor, a step above the
average cafe.

I went inside and took the last table, which was
jammed into one corner of the cafe. The room was
crowded, so I figured either the grub was good or the
cowpokes were partial to wooden floors. I laid my
slouch hat in the chair next to me and ran my fingers
through my short-cut hair, glad that I had visited to
the barber before I left D.C. If this weather was any
indication, we were in for an early spring.

With all of the grace of a whitetail fawn, a young
blond waitress bustled around, taking orders, returning
with plates heaped with steaming beans and beef,
which as in most western cafes, was the only grub
available. I didn't pay her much attention, but in the
one glimpse I did get when she turned sideways, I saw
she wore a bright smile on her face. Strangely enough,
there was something familiar about her, but I couldn't
figure what it was.

When it was my turn, she hurried up to me while glancing over her shoulder and carrying on a laughing conversation with one of the cowpokes at another table. "Hi, there, cowboy. What'll you . . ." She froze. Her mouth dropped open in disbelief.

"Ben?" she whispered in disbelief. "Ben, is that you?"

Her question slammed me between the eyes. I studied her face a moment, the green eyes, the little turned-up nose, the hair like corn silk. "I . . . I'm sorry, Miss, but—"

"Ben, it's me, Susan, Morning Star."

I couldn't believe my eyes. The woman was Susan. She was alive! "*Sons-ee-ah-ray*," I cried out, using her Apache name out of habit. I jumped to my feet. She cried out my Apache name, *Ah-han-day*, and threw herself into my arms, both of us laughing and crying, each surprised and thrilled the other still lived.

The cafe patrons looked at us curiously, but we paid them no attention.

The cafe closed its doors at nine. Nervously flipping the rawhide loop on and off the hammer of my Colt, I waited for Susan. She came out, and we hugged again.

Then, arm in arm, like brother and sister, we strolled down the boardwalk, paying no attention to anyone else. I had eleven years' worth of questions and eleven years' worth of news for her. But within two minutes, we were standing in the middle of the street glaring at each other.

"You . . . you're going to do what?" she asked, disbelief evident in her voice.

"I'm going after *Nah-kay-yen*. To find out the truth.

I don't believe the stories about him, but Washington is convinced he's the leader of a renegade band of Apaches. I've got to find him and prove them wrong. If I don't, the government will send in an army, and Arizona will run red with blood. And *Nah-kay-yen* will be the first one they go after.''

She stared at me like I was a Gila monster ready to crawl up her arm. "But you can't arrest him. He's your brother.''

"That's exactly why I'm here. Anyone else comes in, they come in shooting. I told you, I don't believe Keen Sighted is part of this band. I've got to find him. I've got to prove he is innocent, and he'll have to help me." But, I wondered to myself, what would I do if I discovered he was guilty, that he was responsible for the savagery terrifying Arizona?

Ears burning, I pushed the idea out of my mind, ashamed of harboring such a thought about my own brother.

I hoped Susan believed me, but Apache parents bred skepticism into every Apache child, white or red, at an early age, and that skepticism remained an integral part of their life. And Susan had been younger than me when they took us, so the Apache teachings had a better chance of sticking with her.

At first, my explanation soothed her outrage. The frown disappeared from her forehead, and a reluctant smile turned up the edges of her lips. "All right, if that's what you're really trying to do.''

I searched her eyes. "I've known you since I was ten and you were four. Have I ever lied?''

She edged around until she had my face in the yellow glow from one of the saloon windows. "No,'' she finally replied, throwing her arms around my waist and hugging her face to my chest. "It's so wonderful to be with you again. I missed you so much."

A patrol of troopers rode past, followed by a wiry Apache scout wearing a breechcloth and trooper's jacket. He glanced at us.

I paid him only scant attention. "I've missed you too, and I've got an armload of questions anxious to get out." Later, I would tell her about her family in Missouri, but now I wanted to find out about my brother. "Have you seen him lately?"

She looked up at me. "Keen Sighted? No. It's been almost four years."

Before I could ask why, she continued, laying her head back on my chest and tightening her arms about my waist. "Oh, I can't believe you're here. Come on back to the Reverend Beecher's with me. We have a spare room."

Her remarks concerning Keen Sighted puzzled me, but I laughed and hugged her tightly. A strange warmth filled me as I held her. I had no idea I could have been so happy to see anyone. "Thanks, but I've got a room at the hotel."

A becoming pout pursed her lips. "But I want to hear everything you've done."

"Don't worry," I replied. "We'll have all the time in the world. But who's this Reverend Beecher, and what are you doing at his house?"

She ignored my question. "At least, come meet him and his wife, Mary Catherine. I've lived with them since . . ." She hesitated, and her fingers tightening on mine, Susan stopped and looked up at me.

We were past the last building. Only the sickle

moon lit us. Her face shone in the pale light, but her eyes were lost in dark shadows. I saw the frown wrinkling her forehead. "Why, you don't know, do you?" she asked, surprised. "About *Kay-tanh* and the others?" She shook her head. "No, you couldn't."

A chill raced through my body. "Know what?" *Kay-tanh* was my Apache father. His name meant Corn Flower, for as a young man he and his party hid in a cornfield near the large town of Ures in Sonora and succeeded in running off three hundred ponies from the Mexicans. On one occasion *Kay-tanh* was kicked in the face by a mule, which broke and flattened his nose. Then the Mexicans, who lived in deathly fear of him, called him Chato, meaning flat- or pug-nose, a name I much preferred for my father rather than Corn Flower.

Her face crumpled into tears, and she buried it in my chest. "Oh, Ben, I'm so sorry."

Puzzled, I held her in my arms and tried to soothe her, at the same time struggling to keep a rein on my own apprehensions her words had evoked. "What are you talking about? What is there to know about Chato?"

Her sobs subsided. She looked up at me. "I'm sorry, Ben." She drew a deep breath and faced me with the same determined jaw she had thrust out to the Apaches when they captured us twenty years earlier. "Chato is dead. So is Broken Knee. That's when Keen Sighted took up the lance against the white man," she added, falling back into the Apache idiom. "That's why I haven't seen him for so long. It's too dangerous for him to come near Tucson."

The words hit me between the eyes like a singletree.

I forgot all about my other questions as I closed my eyes and fought the tears welling in my eyes and the lump burning in my throat. When Susan and I were brought into the Apache rancheria as children, she was adopted by Colored Beads, and I was adopted by Chato and his favorite wife, Broken Knee, who raised me as their own along with Keen Sighted, Broken Knee's only child.

Two years before I left, the summer Keen Sighted and I became eighteen, Colored Beads's wife had a child, a boy, an *ish-kay-nay* who was a brother to *Sons-ee-ah-ray*.

I asked her about her brother.

"I don't know. I did not find him among the dead, but many ran into the mountains and were there slain." Her gaze fell to the ground. "I never found the *ish-kay-nay*," she whispered.

I stood rigid, unaware of the warm breeze gently blowing over us, unaware of the crickets chirruping, unaware of Susan's consoling words. Instead, I fought against the sudden anger that sprang up inside me, the same blazing, intense anger that had driven the Apache to fight when the first white man invaded Indian land.

I forced the hatred aside and struggled to still the pounding drumbeat vibrating through my blood. Echoing from the depths of my memory, I heard Chato's deep, resonant voice counseling me. "Wait . . . be patient as the hawk. Do not permit anger to throw the sand in your eyes."

Slowly I climbed out of the dark morass of anger, back to the present, to the dark street in Tucson. Susan was looking into my face, her own filled with sympathetic concern. With Apache stoicism, I asked, "How did he die?"

She laced her fingers into mine and tugged me gently after her. "Let's go on to the parsonage. I'll make us some coffee."

Numbed by her revelation, I followed. On the way to the parsonage, she told how on the day of the massacre four years earlier, "I had ridden to another valley in the Cimarron Mountains for blackberries. Midmorning, I heard gunfire. By the time I reached the edge of the forest near the rancheria, the attack was over. Bluecoats were everywhere."

"I hid up in the mountains." She paused. Her voice dropped to a whisper. "I lay on a ledge above the rancheria. I watched the bluecoats carry away their own wounded and then return to shoot every Apache just to make certain they all were dead."

We stopped in the shadows in front of the parsonage, a whitewashed adobe. "What happened to Chato?" I asked again, my voice aching with pain.

She shook her head. She replied in a whisper. "I don't know. I found him outside his wickiup. He lay in the doorway. Broken Knee lay inside."

I winced as the image flashed through my brain. "Did he kill many?" The words burst from my lips of their own volition, my dignity seeking assurance that my father's death was not cheaply bought.

The shadows of the parsonage buried Susan's face deep in its gloom, but I fancied I could see the puzzled frown on her face as she wondered why I should ask such a question. Yet she should have known without wondering. "I don't know. I waited until all the soldiers left before I went down." I had to lean forward to hear her reply.

"You say you did not find the *ish-kay-nay*?"

"No. But he was not among the dead."

"Perhaps he still lives. Was he named?"

Susan nodded. "Yes. He was no longer an *ish-kay-nay*. He was Young Eagle."

"And your father, Colored Beads?"

Her fingers tightened about my hand. I pulled her to me and held her close. I could feel the silent sobs in her small body. "I'm sorry."

After a few moments, she pulled back. With the dogged resiliency of the Apache, she said, "It is over. We must look forward."

We both ducked as the abrupt beating of wings shattered the silence of the night just above our heads. A swooping owl angled sharply away upon recognizing the source of the whispers on which it had dived.

I looked up into the night. The sickle moon lit the mountaintops with a dim glow. I wondered again how many bluecoats Chato took with him. A feeling of consternation suddenly gripped me, for before I had realized the direction of my own thoughts, I found myself hoping that he had killed many bluecoats before he died.

Why should I hope such a thing? Especially against the bluecoats with whom I worked shoulder to shoulder. But, I reminded myself, I grew up Apache. Even eleven years in the white man's world could make no great difference. No one makes such changes quickly.

Her small fingers touched my arm. "Are you all right, Ben?"

"Yes," I replied, smiling down at her. "I'm fine."

I wasn't. I never would be, at least, not as I had been before tonight. But the Apache in me knew that change was imminent, and the white man's blood in my veins assured me that only fools fought against the change. "Any idea why the Army attacked Chato and his people?" I asked.

She ducked her head so her face was hidden from my eyes. But from the sarcasm in her voice, I knew a sneer twisted her lips when she replied, "Always the same, *Ah-han-day*. You know that. The bluecoats search for Apache. They find Apache. So, they kill Apache, guilty or not."

"Nothing changes, huh?"

Susan laughed bitterly. "Nothing changes." She slid her fingers down my arm and gripped my hand. "I buried Chato and Broken Knee next to Colored Beads in a canyon near the rancheria. I buried them all. It took me three days, but I piled rocks high to keep off the coyote and the buzzards. I will show you someday."

I raised my head and looked northeast toward the Cimarron Mountains. "I'd like that."

She reached behind her and opened the door. "Come inside, Ben. Meet the Beechers."

"Not tonight," I replied quickly, pulling her away from the door. She started to argue, but I added, "Tomorrow. You understand?"

Susan squeezed my hand. "Yes," she whispered. "I understand."

I noted with satisfaction that she was still Apache, that she contained her emotions well.

"Ben?"

"Yes."

"What if Keen Sighted was the one who killed this man from Washington?"

I studied her face. I knew the answer before I asked the question. "The truth?"

Her grip about my hand relaxed. "Yes."

Taking a deep breath, I told her the truth. "If Keen Sighted is guilty, he must stand trial. That means I must take him to the bluecoats and put him behind bars. What we all must realize is that today—"

"No!" Susan slung my hand away. "No, you can't. Whatever Keen Sighted has done, he was forced to do it by the bluecoats, by *your* Washington," she said, her last words sharp with sarcasm. "The bluecoats attacked the rancheria. We had done nothing. They surprised us. You can't take Keen Sighted."

"I don't have a choice. This is a job I have to do."

"Are you sure? Or is it one you want to do so the white man will accept you?" she fired back, her words clipped with poorly suppressed rage.

I didn't reply. I couldn't. I should have known she wouldn't understand. No Apache understands another seeking one of his own, just as they did not understand those who served as bluecoat scouts against their own.

But my mission was different. I was not a red man wanting to turn white. I was not against Keen Sighted. I wanted to save his life, by whatever means I could. And who could tell. If I did, then maybe the ranch I had dreamed of for the two—no, now it was the three of us, might still come true. Susan, Keen Sighted, and me—on a ranch of our dreams in Wyoming.

Softly I replied, "This is the only way to help him. You've got to understand."

She stepped back and crossed her arms and tilted

her jaw at me. When I realized she was not going to reply, I continued. "I'm pulling out in the morning. I'll see you when I return."

Her words were icy and cold. "You go through with this, don't bother about coming back. You are no longer Apache," she snapped. She spun on her heel and slammed the door open and banged it shut.

I turned back to the hotel, weighed down by guilt. Her feelings were my own feelings, but someone, somewhere had to make an effort to stop the senseless slaughter, slaughter of the red man as well as the white.

But I asked myself the same question. What if Keen Sighted was guilty? What then? I truly believed him to be innocent, but what if he wasn't? What if he was indeed the leader of this renegade band? What if they were the very ones who murdered John Salmon Cook? Then what would I do?

How the change came about, I don't know, but in the darkness under that dim sickle moon, I felt a thin layer of the white man slip away from me, like a veil of silk sliding off a woman's head. If Keen Sighted were among those guilty, I would do what I had to do, what Chato would have done, without choice. Slowly the ranch of which I had dreamed began to fade. I had wanted to tell Susan of it, but the anger and hurt got in the way.

Chapter Three

When the sun rose next morning, I was squatting on my heels by a small fire on the bank of a tributary of the Santa Cruz River, waiting for my coffee to boil. My forearms rested on my knees, and my hands were clasped in front of me.

The air was clean and fresh, filled with a sharp, tangy fragrance that filtered all of the impurities from your blood and packed your muscles with energy. Just being alive was a blessing. The sun rolled up over the mountains and painted the sky with bold strokes of blazing orange.

I stiffened. I felt vibrations in the ground. When I left the hotel that morning, I stored my boots and donned my moccasins, single-soled Plains gear, which provided not only a tough and durable footwear, but also an additional degree of sensitivity to my surroundings.

Through the soles of my feet, I felt faint reverberations. I remained motionless, but I cut my eyes upstream. Near the bend in the stream, a rabbit burst from a small patch of grama grass along the bank and disappeared into a large cluster of hedgehog cactus, their blooms beginning to open into a brilliant strawberry red.

Without moving my head, I scanned the desert before me. Slowly I reached down and flipped the rawhide loop off the hammer of my .45.

The vibrations intensified. I had been eleven years away from the desert and mountains, and as with all talents, tracking skills grow rusty without use. The best estimate I could make on the approaching party was that it was made up of at least three or four, perhaps as many as eight or nine riders. I muttered a dark oath at my own incompetence. But at least I could tell that they were not galloping their animals, but keeping them in a gentle walking trot, a mile-eating gait utilized to cover as much ground as possible in a given time.

Impatiently I flipped the rawhide loop on and off the hammer of my Colt. An unfamiliar excitement flowed through my veins as I awaited their arrival with anticipation.

Four mounted braves rounded the bend and, without a break in stride, continued toward me. I studied them. One carried a Winchester. Each of the other three rode with his free hand resting on his thigh. All rode with the assured aplomb of the Apache, lazy, uncaring, all poured in the same mold.

Their black hair hung to their shoulders, swept back from dark, flashing eyes by broad headbands of varying colors. They wore muslin breechcloths and leather boots of deerskin, the legs of which flopped about their ankles. Their rugged bodies gave mute evidence of the Apache's bulldog toughness and tenacity.

As they approached, I rose and moved a few steps to my right, making room for them to stop between me and the bank of the stream, which would also face them into the sun.

Ignoring my bait, they halted several yards away. The pungent, barnyard smell of lathered horseflesh rolled forward, swirling about me. The Apache in front smirked as he saw through my ploy. He looked at the bank of the stream, and then the sun, and then back at me. His smirk broadened. I shrugged and allowed a small grin to play over my own lips, a casual bantering between enemies.

But my eyes kept returning to the brave with the unleathered Winchester. He had his finger on the trigger, but, for the moment, the rifle hung at his side, the muzzle pointed at the ground.

The four of them studied me as I did them. I knew how their minds worked. Here was a white man, probably with many valuables. If they thought they could kill me, they would, but they also saw the revolver on my hip, which forced them to hesitate and wonder. How good was this white man with the gun?

The Apache was not a fool. As the white man, he played the odds of the game. If they were in his favor, he acted. If not—there would always be another time, another game, another hand to be dealt.

I tossed in a chip to swing the odds in my favor. ''I am *Ah-han-day*, son of Chato. I have been to the land of the Father of the Bluecoats.'' I made a sweeping gesture with my left hand to the east without taking my eyes from their faces.

Intrigued, the leader urged his pony a few steps closer. ''That is easy to say. I think perhaps you are of those who pay the bluecoats to look for the *orahay*.''

''I do not lie,'' I replied, my words testy, my tone suggesting offense at his remarks. ''Broken Knee was my mother. My brother is *Nah-kay-yen*. The Mexicans call him Keen Sighted.''

Out of the corner of my eye, I saw the Winchester move. Instinctively my hand flashed to the revolver, and before any of the Apaches could move, I had dropped into a crouch and had the muzzle of the .45 trained on them. ''Leave the rifle where it is,'' I said slowly and emphatically.

All four froze, but their eyes bored into mine.

I glanced at the first Apache. ''I pay bluecoats nothing. I am no seeker of gold. I am Mimbre Apache. I wish no trouble with my brothers just because I was born white. That was not of my choosing, but I travel with a purpose. No one will stop me. If I must, I will kill you and leave you here for the buzzards.'' I paused to let my words soak in.

The first Apache nodded. ''You must be a great warrior to be so certain of your strength.''

''And you do not appear a fool who wishes to test my strength.''

The first Apache grinned and clasped his hands in front of his body, the back of the left one down, indicating peace. The Apache with the Winchester shoved the carbine in its boot. The first one continued.

"I am Strong Swimmer. He . . ." He gestured to the one with the Winchester. "He is Black Wolf." Strong Swimmer named the other two, but I focused my attention on Black Wolf. Here was a man who was the embodiment of his name. He bore watching. "We are Nedni, from the tribe of Chief Juh," Strong Swimmer added.

A grin came unbidden to my lips.

Strong Swimmer frowned.

"Do not be offended," I replied, returning the .45 to its holster. "The mention of Chief Juh gives me pleasant memories. As youths, Keen Sighted and I visited his tribe. We were but young and foolish boys, *ish-kay-nays*, handling the remuda for the older braves." I nodded to the next range of mountains to the west. "Is Juh still in the Baboquivaris?"

A smile ticked up one edge of Strong Swimmer's lips. With the exception of Black Wolf, the frowns on the faces of the others faded. "The bluecoats have become like irritating flies. Juh has moved to the Sierra Madres."

"In Mexico?"

"Yes. Was that not wise? Now the bluecoats cannot follow."

I grinned back at him. "Juh was always a wise chief. What of the Federales?"

Strong Swimmer grinned broadly, revealing a set of even white teeth. He made a throwaway gesture with his hand. "They are less than nothing to us."

Black Wolf interrupted. "Tell the white man no more. How do we know he speaks the truth?" His jaw was set, and he glared at me with eyes cold as black ice.

A heavy tension suddenly fell over us.

I returned his stare. I knew what I must do. "I have said I do not lie. If Black Wolf does not choose to believe me, so be it. But, if Black Wolf questions my words, then I say he is a fool, without the sense of a rabbit."

Black Wolf stiffened in his saddle. His hand slid off his thigh to the butt of his Winchester.

I remained as I was, loose and relaxed, but every muscle in my body was ready to spring into action, packed with tingling anticipation, pumped to bursting with the expectation of potential battle. The thrill of my first skirmish as a youth against the Mexicans flooded over me, filling me with nervous excitement.

Although I was not aware of it at the time, I now know the confrontation with Black Wolf stripped another tenuous layer of the white man's culture away from me, bringing my Apache upbringing nearer the surface.

Without taking my eyes from his, I spoke softly, almost gently. "Black Wolf will be dead if his fingers touch the rifle."

His hand hesitated. He tried to bluff me, but he saw the look of the wolf in my eyes, and he knew I meant what I said. He sat back in his saddle, and his shoulders slumped, but his malevolent eyes continued to burn a hole in me.

The tension faded.

I remained wary, but I extended my hospitality. I pointed to the coffee. "There is not much, but you are welcome."

None of the four moved. Nor did I. For what seemed like hours, we stared at each other. Finally,

Strong Swimmer nodded. ''I have heard of *Ah-han-day*. Have you remembered any of your long journey yet?''

His question surprised me, but it shouldn't have. While there arc many separate Apache tribes, they communicate readily. During the years I lived with them, my story spread through the land of the Apache, among whom there are no secrets. They all knew of my capture, of my loss of memory, of all that was important about me to know, and they noted these facts with my name, *Ah-han-day*, in English, A Long Way, to denote the long journey or distance I would travel in my life without knowledge of where I had been or what I had done before the Apache.

''No. I know nothing before the Summer of the Antelope, when I came to live with Chato and Broken Knee.''

''The name is good,'' he said. ''*Ah-han-day*, A Long Way.'' He paused again, then made a fist and pressed it against his broad chest. ''Strong Swimmer is friend to A Long Way.''

I nodded. ''I am fortunate to have such a friend.''

''Why is A Long Way here?''

''To find my brother, Keen Sighted.''

Black Wolf frowned.

I continued, wanting to be as open and honest as possible. ''My brother has been wrongly accused of murdering a man, an important man among the blue-coats. The Great Father in Washington will send an army after my brother if I cannot prove he is innocent.''

Strong Swimmer grunted. ''You believe Keen Sighted is innocent?''

"Yes," I replied emphatically. "I know my brother. We grew up together. We even fought the Federales, and escaped from the bluecoats together. Yes, I believe he is innocent of this crime."

With a satisfied nod, Strong Swimmer wheeled his pony around. He looked over his shoulder at me and grinned, then dug his heels into the pony's flanks. As one, the four riders headed back upstream.

Puzzling over the seekers of gold of whom they spoke, I watched until they disappeared around the first bend. Who could blame their anger if the bluecoats were permitting treaties to be violated? I shook my head and turned back to my boiling coffee. That would have to be someone else's headache. I had enough to handle with my present assignment.

The rich chicory aroma of fresh coffee mixed with the clean smell of morning air overpowered the fading smell of horse. I poured a cup of the black liquid, thick enough to walk on. Some folks figure my coffee is too strong, but during my service in the Union Army, I acquired a taste for coffee strong enough to curl a wagon tongue.

For several minutes, I remained in a squat, sipping my coffee and watching the metamorphosis of the Arizona desert from a drab and cold barrens into a breathtaking panorama filled with brilliantly hued wildflowers and majestic saguaro, some hundreds of years old, stretching their arms to the blue skies above. In the distance, a coyote wailed as it made its way back to its lair.

Memories flooded back, but I shoved them aside. I had a job to do, and the sooner I got about it, the sooner it would be over—one way or the other.

I dumped the coffee grounds in the sand and packed my gear. After tightening the cinch and checking the rigging on the roan, I mounted and headed west. If G Troop was where the sheriff said, I had about another three- or four-hour ride ahead of me.

Four hours later, I reined up on the crest of a small mesa. A shallow basin a couple miles wide lay before me. Halfway across sprawled the bluecoat camp, an unorderly collection of tents, wickiups, and lean-tos along the east bank of a narrow stream.

I surveyed the layout, taking in the lack of organization of the camp. The back of my neck prickled. I hoped the shabby camp was no indication of its commanding officer. For my plan to succeed, I might need his help. But the closer I drew to the camp, the more concerned I became.

A young sentry escorted me to the captain's quarters, one of two wall tents facing each other with a canvas fly stretched between their entrances to form a small arbor.

I introduced myself and showed the commanding officer my orders, which were very explicit. A lieutenant slouched in a chair in the corner of the tent, a half-filled glass of whiskey in his hand.

An obese, weak-chinned man with bushy porkchop sideburns covering fat jaws, Captain R. Albert Simpson read my orders and then glared at me with his watery green eyes. In a squeaky voice, he said, "It doesn't say who you are working for."

I failed to understand his statement. "Sir?"

He waved the orders in the air. "This doesn't say what outfit you are attached to."

"That's right, Captain. I'm attached to no one. I'm reporting to you as a courtesy between my department and the war department to ask for your assistance in setting up a meeting with some Apaches."

Captain Simpson shook his head and gave the lieutenant a sneer. In his lilting, high-pitched voice, he asked, "What do you think about that, Lieutenant Irons? Your grandfather was a Confederate general. What would he have done if someone reported and announced that he was attached to no unit, that he was on his own?" He picked up his own whiskey and gulped it down.

Lieutenant Irons, a skinny, sallow-faced man, shrugged. I had the feeling that he had no more idea what point Captain Simpson was trying to make than I did.

"That's the problem with this army," continued the captain, his face florid with alcohol. "I've said it before, and I'll say it again. No one in this army knows who he works for. That's wrong. Everyone works for someone. That's the only way to maintain discipline and order. Everyone must work for someone. But does the Army listen? No. They just keep going about their blundering ways like they were going to a birthday party."

Now, I probably would never win any medals for brains, but after his last remarks, I figured out right fast exactly why Captain R. Albert Simpson was patrolling one of the least desirable commands in the country. He was an arrogant and short-sighted man in camp, and in all probability, a less than dedicated and enterprising warrior on the battlefield.

But I said nothing of my thoughts to him. "I am a

member of the Secret Service, Captain. I am not military. My purpose here is to seek your assistance, one government agency to another.''

Simpson tossed my orders on his desk and snorted. He poured another glass of whiskey. ''I don't see where I have much choice to disagree, do you, Mr. Moore?''

I tried to pacify him. ''Yes, sir, you do. You can choose not to aid me.''

He jumped to his feet and jabbed a fat forefinger at me. ''Ah, ha, just what I thought. You've been sent out here to test me.'' He hefted his bulky body around to face Lieutenant Irons. ''Someone wrote a letter, William. About me. Someone complained.'' He pounded the air with his fist like he was banging on a door. His great belly, which hung over his belt, shook like jelly.

Lieutenant Irons shook his head. He replied in a deep, resonant voice that did not seem to fit with his thin, anemic frame. ''Not me, Albert.''

''You have it all wrong, Captain,'' I broke in. ''No one wrote any letters. I told you the truth. I've been sent to meet with some Apaches. I need your help.''

He glared at me, but his bottom lip was quivering. ''All right, Mr. Secret Service. What aid do you seek?''

''One of your scouts. I wish for him to go to the Apache Keen Sighted and tell him that his brother, A Long Way, wishes to meet with him.''

''His brother? I thought you said you wanted to meet with him?''

Lieutenant Irons leaned forward, his emaciated and elongated face wrinkled with a curious scowl.

"I am his brother, Captain."

Captain Simpson took a step back. Instinctively he reached for his sidearm hanging from a tent pole.

"Hold it, Captain. I'm a white man, and I am who I say." I didn't want to say more, to reveal any details, for my life is my own private business, but this was one instance, I decided, where I needed to explain how I had come to be just where I was.

"When I was a child, the Indians attacked and killed everyone on the wagon train my family was in. Best I can figure, they left me for dead. When I woke up, I couldn't remember anything. After burying everyone, I picked up a family Bible on the ground by the nearest wagon and started walking. A couple days later, a man named John Leslie found me. Him and his wife and daughter were headed for the copper mines at Santa Rita, but we never made it. Two days later, the Apache killed them, but they took me and the little girl to live with them. I remained there for ten summers."

I paused. Captain Simpson was eyeing me suspiciously, but the lieutenant was mesmerized by every word I said.

"The Apache home that took me in was that of Chato, and Keen Sighted was Chato's son. We grew up together as brothers. I know him, and I think I can get him to come in without any more killing."

The tent grew silent. Captain Simpson broke the silence. "Why aren't you still with them?" The skepticism in his voice was obvious.

"When I was about twenty, Chato, who was a very wise man, gave me the Bible I carried when the Apache took me. He thought the names in it would be important to me, so I went to Pennsylvania to look up my family.'' I hesitated, the disappointing memories filling me with a sad loneliness again. ''I found the family, but it turned out the Bible was not mine, but belonged to one of the other families that was murdered on the train.''

Captain Simpson flopped down in his chair. The joints creaked from the great weight of his corpulent body. He looked up at me, a crooked grin on his face. I couldn't prove it, but I sensed he took great delight in saying, ''So you never found out who you were.''

The imperious tone in his voice rankled me. I ignored the question. ''What I need is one of your scouts to find Keen Sighted and tell him that at sunrise, four days from now, I will be waiting where this stream at your door meets the Santa Cruz River to the north.''

He laced his fat fingers together across his broad belly and in his most confidential tone, said, ''How many troopers will we need?''

I shook my head. ''No troopers, Captain. And no 'we,' just me.''

He leaned forward in his chair, his bloated face growing red. ''That is not sound strategy, Mr. Moore. I'm afraid I must insist. Your certain demise will place a blemish on my record.''

The white man's abysmal ignorance of the Apache never ceased to amaze me. Simpson was no exception. ''Captain, I mean no offense, but there is no strategy that will take advantage of the Apache. Such has been obvious for years. I can do what needs to be done all by myself.''

He shook his head, his fat jowls shaking. ''Absolutely not. As commander of this district, I must forbid such a move. When you go to meet this Apache, my troops will accompany you.''

We stared at each other for several seconds. He was as stubborn as he was fat, and only drastic action would move him from his decision. So I gave it a shot. ''That being the case, Captain, all I can do then is return to Washington.'' I nodded to him. ''If you'll excuse me, there's plenty daylight. I can reach Tucson by midnight if I leave now.''

His heavy-lidded eyes opened wide in surprise, but he quickly recovered. He cleared his throat. ''Are you sure such a decision is wise, Mr. Moore? After all, if you were sent out here to—''

I interrupted him. ''The decision is not mine, Captain. The decision is Washington's. If at all possible, I follow their orders. If for some reason, I am unable to carry out my orders, then I am to return.'' I was stretching the interpretation of my orders, but I didn't figure Captain Simpson would risk second-guessing me. He was thinking of himself, of his own career, and the implication in my words was obvious. Either he did it my way, or his career, what pitifully little of it remained, would be swept away in the first dust devil that blew past.

If looks could kill, I would have been carried from his tent, but finally, he consented. ''I misunderstood your orders, Mr. Moore. My apologies. Certainly, whatever I can do to assist you, I will. All you have to do is ask.''

''Thank you, Captain,'' I replied, my words as sugar sweet as his, and just as hypocritical. ''All I need is a scout, and then if I am successful, and Keen

Sighted comes in with me, we will also need a safe place for him to stay until a trial can be arranged.''

''And this trial. Where is it to be, Fort Bowie or Fort Prescott? Prescott is the Southern Command headquarters. Or have you decided?''

I held my temper in control. ''That's not up to me, Captain. Washington will decide.''

Simpson's pig eyes squinted. ''A trial's too good for those savages. They should all be shot on sight.''

''But you don't know if he's guilty or not.''

''If he's guilty.'' Simpson hefted his bulky body to his feet. ''Why, man, you know he's guilty. All of those Indians are nothing but dastardly murderers. They all should be punished with fire and brimstone.''

He paused. A thoughtful look came over him as his rabid little mind grabbed hold of an idea. He arched an eyebrow at Lieutenant Irons and scratched his right sideburn. ''All right, Mr. Moore. You shall have your scout.''

''Thank you, Captain,'' I replied. ''With your permission, I'll set up camp upstream. I plan on pulling out early in the morning.''

He nodded to Lieutenant Irons. ''The lieutenant here will accompany you to your camp and see to all your needs. Is that clear, Lieutenant Irons?''

Like a fleeting shadow, a faint smirk raced across Irons's face. ''Yes, sir,'' he replied, his voice resounding with military assertiveness.

The lieutenant looked at him, and I caught the look that passed between them. Captain Simpson might be willing to help me, but I knew that any help he gave would only be because somehow he would benefit even more than me. He and the lieutenant were two men I would watch carefully.

I paused outside the tent, awaiting Lieutenant Irons. From inside, Captain Simpson's squeaky voice whispered, ''Just think, William. What a feather in my cap if we had this renegade's trial right here. Such a coup could possibly get me released from this infernal pit called Arizona Territory. Nothing would suit me better.''

I shook my head at his grandiose scheme. Washington would never consider a trial here. Sooner or later, Captain Albert Simpson would find that out for himself.

That night, a sullen Apache scout by the name of Big Bow showed up as I sipped on a final cup of coffee. I heard him approaching from the darkness. When I looked around, he stood hipshot on the edge of the firelight, a battered Springfield cradled in the crook of his arm.

Neither of us spoke for a moment. I broke the silence. ''The captain send you?''

His dark eyes glittered in the firelight as he nodded, a frown on his dark face.

I gestured to the coffeepot, but he remained motionless, swaying slightly on his feet. ''You know the Mimbre Apache, Keen Sighted?''

He gave a brief nod.

''Can you find him?''

Another nod.

''I have a message for him. You are to carry it.''

''If I choose,'' he replied haughtily, shifting his weight to his other foot.

I looked at him carefully, hiding the frown his

words evoked, puzzling at his obvious hostility and insolence. I rose and stepped over the small fire to stand in front of him.

Then I realized what was behind his arrogance. He had been drinking, and he blamed me for cutting his alcoholic binge short. I wouldn't say he was falling-down drunk, but he was high enough to parley with a passing eagle. "That is not as the captain told me. You were sent to carry out an order."

He arched an eyebrow warily. "What is it the man from Washington wishes with Keen Sighted?"

I fired back my reply, my words sharp and cold as the winter wind. "That is of no concern to you. You are to carry a message. That is all."

The scout suppressed his anger at my sharp words. "He will be hard to find."

It was my turn to become angry. "Captain Simpson says you are his best scout. Perhaps I should find a Paiute squaw to carry the message. Perhaps she will not let the whiskey cloud her thinking."

His wiry body stiffened, and for a moment, I thought I had pushed him too hard. But I had grown weary of his crawfishing. Very deliberately, I poured my coffee on the fire and stood to face him. "Either you do as I ask, or return to the captain. I do not care. I will find another to carry my word."

He glared at me, and I returned his look. To an Apache, face is everything. To his way of thinking, if I sent him back, he would be disgraced in the eyes of the captain. His eyes narrowed, and he pressed his fist against his chest. "I will go. I alone can find the one you seek," he said, his words frosted with resentment. "I, Big Bow, can follow the grasshopper over the mountain,'' he added, making a rising and falling gesture with his hand to symbolize a mountain. ''I can find anyone *you* want,'' he concluded, his words clipped, his tone patronizing.

He was stretching the truth a little, at least about the grasshopper, but now he was willing to carry my message to Keen Sighted. ''Good.'' Then I gave him a figurative pat on the back. ''Perhaps the captain was right when he said that Big Bow is his greatest scout.''

As with the white man, temperament in the Apache differs. Big Bow possessed a mercurial disposition, wildly fluctuating in his emotions, for in the next moment, his frown evaporated, and his thin face broke into a wrinkled wreath of smiles, revealing a set of even white teeth. ''Captain Simpson will be proud of Big Bow.''

I nodded. ''And if Big Bow does his job well, the captain will give him a medal,'' I said, speaking of him as if he were another person.

Big Bow beamed. ''Do not worry. I will find Keen Sighted and give him your message.''

''Good. Tell him that I, A Long Way . . .'' I pointed to myself. ''His brother, wishes to speak with him in four mornings where this stream leaves the big river to the north.''

If learning I was brother to Keen Sighted surprised Big Bow, he covered it well. His face remained impassive. He nodded. For a moment, he studied me, then turned back to camp and disappeared into the darkness beyond the firelight.

The darkness drew closer as the small fire died down. I sat on my haunches, peering into the darkness where Big Bow had disappeared. I was uneasy about him. Like many men, both Apache and white, he seemed to drift with the wind, whichever way would most benefit him. I was placing myself in a ticklish enough spot just being out there alone, but when you toss in an uncertain factor like Big Bow, it seemed like the house suddenly had all the odds in its favor.

Banking my fire, I rolled into my soogan. Ten minutes later, the soft thud of pony hooves passed close to my camp and disappeared in the darkness to the west. Just before I slipped into a restless slumber, I thought about Lieutenant Irons.

I had heard of an Irons in the war, a Confederate general. It was hard to believe he and this lieutenant were related. General Irons was a soldier of whom either side could have been mighty proud. I remember the trouble he gave the Federals at the Second Bull Run. From all I heard, the bluecoats were right happy when nighttime came, and the wildcat they called a general returned to his lair.

But this one, the grandson . . . I shook my head. "Yep," I muttered to myself as I turned over and tugged the blankets around my neck. "This appears to be one case where the apple fell a mighty long way from the tree."

Chapter Four

The journey upstream was uneventful, even pleasant, for late winter and early spring in Arizona Territory were my favorite times. And now I once again enjoyed the clean, crisp morning air as well as the sweltering afternoons when the blazing sun boiled the sweat from my body just as quickly as Indian steam lodges sweated the poison from a man's veins.

The sweetness of the desert air made me forget the stench of the city, the reek of mobs, the fetor of civilization. Gazing across the sweeping desert to the blue mountains, I tingled with anticipation and excitement. The cactus splashed the countryside with brilliant bursts of red as blossoms opened to the warming sun. Not to be outdone, the giant saguaros displayed their own large white blooms in counterpoint to the sanguine flowers of the cactus. In the distance, the soft yellow of the paloverde trees provided occasional clumps of eye-pleasing contrast in the colorful panorama.

The intense heat rising from the desert stirred the air, bringing in the usual late-afternoon breezes. I shivered as the chilled perspiration cooled my body.

Reaching the Santa Cruz in midafternoon of the third day, I saw no sense in attempting to hide my camp in any of the nearby shallow arroyos, for I had been watched ever since I left the bivouac area. Once or twice, I caught a fleeting glimpse of one of the watchers, but as quickly as they appeared, they dropped out of sight.

Taking my time, I set up camp and laid a fire in the shade of a willow brake near the river and put water on to boil. While the water boiled, I opened a tin of beans and set it in the sand at the edge of the fire.

While coffee perked and beans warmed, I cut an armload of willow branches, wrist thick and about three feet in length. A fish trap. Shedding my moccasins, I waded into the river and constructed a rectangular trap in a narrow race between two boulders.

The front of the trap was shaped like a funnel. Once trapped, the fish seldom fought against the current, staying instead in the bottom of the trap. It was a sound trap, easily fabricated and just as easily disassembled. Tomorrow's breakfast would be fresh trout.

I hesitated, trying to picture the meeting with Keen Sighted. Would he treat me as a brother? Would he make the sign? Or would he consider me just another white man?

"Well," I muttered, turning back to the small fire. "You can't do anything about that until it happens, so just get on with the business at hand."

After downing the can of beans and draining the coffee down to the dregs, I rolled into my soogan. I lay awake until long after dark, staring at the starry heavens above, remembering my youth in this country. Finally, I slept. I dreamed well that night, knowing that Keen Sighted and his braves were nearby.

Something awakened me early the next morning. Instantly alert, I sat up and glanced at the Big Dipper. Four o'clock, maybe five. I strained my ears for whatever had disturbed me, but all I heard were the sounds of the night, the soft brushing of the willow leaves, the chirrup of crickets, an occasional rabbit squeal, and the gentle wind soughing through the sage and mesquite, rattling the brittlebush.

I lay back, keeping my ears tuned for any out-of-place sound. Slowly the darkness overhead grew lighter, and the stars began to fade into the coming daylight. I rose with the false dawn and stirred up the fire and tossed some kindling on it.

A restlessness came over me, the anticipation of seeing my brother after eleven years. He was out there, probably watching me at this very moment. He would come in when he was ready, not before.

After drawing water from the river, I put coffee on to boil while I removed four fat trout from the trap, leaving the others just in case his whole party wanted breakfast. I butterflied the four trout down the middle and staked them on spits around the campfire for my guests.

While the coffee boiled and the fish sizzled, I retired to the river where I managed to scrape off the last three days' growth of beard without taking off too much of my skin. This was one of the many times that

I wished I had more Indian in me and less hair on my face.

I stared at my reflection in the still backwater of the river, knowing Keen Sighted was out there. What was he thinking as he watched me shave? Would he remember our youth? Or had the last years hardened him against all white men?

Could I convince him to return with me? If he was still the man I had grown up with, then I knew I could. But men do change—often not of their own choosing.

I turned back to the fire and jerked to a halt.

Before the small fire, his eyes fixed on me, squatted Keen Sighted. He was larger, bulkier than I remembered. His shoulders were broader, his arms rippled with wiry muscle. A crooked grin curled his thin lips.

Sliding my knife back into its sheath, I grinned. His smile tightened, and he rose to meet me as I hurried to him. We stopped a couple feet apart and looked at each other. He shook his head. "Living among the bluecoats has not helped. Your face still frightens the deer."

I started to throw my arms about him, but he seemed to have erected a barrier between us, nothing I could pinpoint, but one that still existed. I grinned despite the sudden apprehension I felt. "And yours still makes the crow fly away." My grin broadened. I hoped the humor between us would thaw the icy barrier he had erected.

My words didn't faze him, so I added, "We are both older and uglier."

He replied somberly. "And wiser." He laid his hand on his side, and I saw there an ugly white scar the size of a cactus petal.

We stared into each other's eyes for several moments. My gaze flicked past him briefly. Three Apache watched casually from a nearby arroyo, alert for any sign of ambush.

I broke the awkward tension between us. ''Sit. I will pour us coffee. There is food.'' I nodded to my blanket and reached for the pot. I left the decision to him as to whether he would offer any to his followers.

Keen Sighted glanced around, then crossed his legs and lowered his body to the ground and picked a spit of fish. I handed him a cup and sat by his side.

We sat without speaking, sipping at the thick black coffee and nibbling absently at the fish as the sun rose.

''I have missed the sunrises,'' I said softly as a tiny sparrow swooped down and landed by the river's edge. As we both watched, the tiny bird dipped its beak in the water, then looked up, jerking its head from side to side nervously, before dipping into the water again.

High overhead, a red-tailed hawk circled. The small brown sparrow repeated the act several times, each time growing more and more nervous as the hawk circled lower and lower.

Suddenly, the sparrow sped away, staying low over the lazily rolling river until the tiny bird reached a stand of willows on the far bank below a high bluff. At the last moment when it appeared the sparrow would bypass the willows, the bird threw out its wings and cut sharply to the right and disappeared into the willows.

''The sparrow is wise,'' Keen Sighted said. ''He knows where danger cannot go.'' He tossed the remainder of his uneaten fish away.

I looked around at my brother. "There is no danger here. This is just like the willows."

He looked around at me, his black eyes expressing no emotion. One side of his lips twisted into a faint sneer. "My brother has been with the white man for many summers. Perhaps he now thinks the Apache are children who will believe whatever he wishes them to believe."

I frowned and tossed my fish to the sand between my feet. "What is it you are telling me?" I touched a finger to my forehead. "I do not think with the wisdom of the owl this morning. You are speaking of something of which I know nothing."

His thick brows knit in a frown of his own. "You are not a bluecoat who has come to lie to us?"

"No," I replied.

"But you have come from the man in Washington?"

Then I understood why he was so distant, so cool. I understood, but that he should think I was here to betray him drove a sharp knife into my chest. "Yes, I come from him, but to help my people, to help you. To stop this killing."

He arched a single eyebrow. "Many have come before you to speak the same words."

While his reaction was slight, the anger it created in me was large. I glared at him. "I do not lie. That, you know. There are questions to be answered, but when the answers are given, all will be over. All will be satisfied."

Keen Sighted realized that I had directed my words at him. A flash of anger darkened his face, but just as quickly, disappeared as a faint sneer arched his thick eyebrows.

I turned my eyes back to the fire and sipped my coffee, which had now lost its taste.

A long silence ensued. I tried to still the anger his almost insignificant gesture and skepticism had ignited. He was as stubborn and suspicious as he had always been, even as a youth. More than once, we had fought because of his suspicions, most of which ended up being unfounded. While we sat, the remaining two fish burned to a crisp and fell in blackened flakes to the ground.

Keen Sighted broke the silence. "Since you have been gone, the white man's lies have filled the air like the stars in the sky. You are the first white man to whom I have spoken since the Moon of the Harvest many years past."

I nodded, reaching out and pouring the dregs of my coffee on the fire. "Once I was Apache to you," I replied, stung by his explanation. "Not just a white man."

He cleared his throat. "You are still Apache."

"You do not treat me as such. You treat me as an enemy, slipping into my camp while my back is turned. You speak with distrust in your voice. Is that how one brother greets another?"

He tilted his chin. The muscles in his jaw rippled beneath the skin as he clenched and unclenched his teeth. As all Apaches, Keen Sighted was sensitive to a strict observation of family obligations and courtesies. "You have been away for many summers. I believed you had forgotten your family."

I laughed. He was searching for a way to save face,

and rather than dispute his last remarks, I salved his conscience. "You should know, my brother, that A Long Way will never forget his Apache family. But I wonder if you have not," I added, hoping to shift him to the defensive.

He cocked his head and stared at me. "What do you mean?"

"Morning Star. She is in Tucson. You have made no effort to see her in these four years. She wonders about you. She wonders if you have thrown her aside."

A look of disbelief spread over his face. "Morning Star lives? I believed that she had been slain as the others when the bluecoats attacked the rancheria."

I curled my lip. "And you did not go back and search for those who were slain? You ran like the rabbit?"

His eyes glittered, and the muscles in his broad jaws stood out like split cordwood. He refused to answer my questions directly as he explained. "I met Standing Bear. I rode with him. I followed him to the Madres where we spent the winter with Juh. Then we returned in the spring and drove the white men from Apache land. We took our revenge for Chato and Broken Knee." His lips folded down into a grimace. I could imagine the dark roads over which his memory was leading him.

I laid my hand on his arm. "We are brothers. If trust cannot be between us, then where can it be?"

Keen Sighted stared at the small fire with a blazing intensity in his own eyes. Slowly the hardness in them faded. A wry grin curled his lips. With a quick flip of his hand, he tossed the remainder of his coffee on the fire and rose to his feet. He looked down at me. "Come," he said. "We will return to my rancheria. There we will drink mescal and feast on venison."

I rose and stood eye to eye with him. The tension between us had disappeared. "Good," I said, laying my hand on his shoulder.

His face clouded with indecision. I knew there was more he wished to say. "What troubles you?"

"I . . ." He paused, searching for the right words. When he continued, his words were soft and halting. "To . . . to explain is difficult. Had you lived in our wickiups these last summers, then you would understand why we doubt the white man. We have been told nothing but lies. When Big Bow came to me with your words, I first thought the bluecoats were laying a snare for me like a rabbit. And like the foolish rabbit is frozen by the stare of the snake, so I was frozen to the feelings in my own heart. I have come to believe all whites were the same. That is why I acted as I did, but I should have remembered my brother was different." He hesitated. His eyebrows knit in a remorseful frown.

His words struck a sad chord in my own heart. What deceits must have been played out to create such distrust in the minds of such an honorable man?

He stared into my eyes with earnest petition.

I grinned. "I understand." I changed the subject. "You have venison in your camp?" I picked up the coffeepot and poured the remainder of the coffee over the fire as I continued, poking fun at him. "Or do I have to kill it?" Memories of our deer and antelope hunts came rushing back. I remembered the feel of the antelope skin draped over my shoulders and tingle of anticipation as the graceful animals drew near, curious of the red cloth we tied to the bloom of a yucca or the spidery leg of an ocotillo.

His lips parted in a broad smile. He responded with heavy sarcasm. "As *ish-kay-nays*, I was always the one who brought the venison to the wickiup of Chato."

The mention of our father's name subdued our laughter. I looked into his eyes, wanting to ask the question I had asked of Susan.

I caught a movement out of the corner of my eye from the top of the bluff across the river. Suddenly, the silence of the morning exploded, and the whine of a slug whistled past my ear.

In the brief moment before the second shot, the growing warmth in Keen Sighted's eyes turned to ice. He glared at me.

At the same instant, I shoved him aside. "Run!" I yelled as the boom of a Springfield Trapdoor filled the air.

A club banged against the back of my head, and a veil of darkness swept over me as I crumpled to the ground. The last I saw of Keen Sighted, he was zig-zagging across the prairie toward one of the shallow arroyos.

Chapter Five

I stumbled back into consciousness, squeezing my eyes shut against the pounding in my head, the intensity of which increased as I became more fully awake. Slowly I opened my eyes.

I lay beneath a canopy of canvas stretched between four poles guyed to stakes. I blinked my eyes slowly and sat up, gingerly touching my fingers to the back of my head. I winced. I had a knot the size of a goose egg.

"You were lucky, Mr. Moore," said a deep voice. "Another inch, and we'd be burying you."

I had lived through enough hangovers to know better than to jerk my head around abruptly. I cut my eyes up to the speaker. It was Lieutenant Irons. I tried to think. What in the blazes was the Army doing here?

Struggling to my feet, I held to one of the corner poles for support and tried to focus my eyes on the lieutenant. Angry questions cut through the fog in my brain, trying to sort through the jumble of confused thoughts tumbling around in my skull.

"What . . . what are you doing here?" I looked past him and saw a troop of cavalry loitering nearby. "What are all of you doing here?" I demanded, clenching my teeth. "I promised Keen Sighted I would come alone."

Lieutenant Irons dropped his gaze to the ground. His elongated face reddened. Before he could reply, Captain Simpson broke in. "You don't show much gratitude for a man whose life has just been saved."

I shook my head, and wished I hadn't. It exploded like a keg of black powder. I looked around at him slowly. Several officers stood behind him, watching curiously. "Saved?" I choked out. "From what?"

Simpson hefted his portly belly around and made a sweeping gesture to the south. "From the savages. In case you were unaware, a horde of savages was hiding in that gully over there."

Several of the officers nodded their agreement.

Glaring at the captain, I fought to keep a rein on my temper, but it was as hard as tying a bow on the tail of a greased pig. "Horde? Keen Sighted brought three braves with him. Three braves don't make a horde."

Simpson shook his head emphatically and gestured to Big Bow and a handful of Apache scouts standing nearby, listening to our exchange. "Our scouts reported a large band of Apaches hiding back in the hills. It was obvious that renegade Apache was going to lead you into an ambush."

"Ambush?" I stared at him in stunned disbelief, my

throbbing skull forgotten. "There was no ambush. There was not going to be any ambush, you st . . ." I bit off my words and tightened my grip on my anger. "Do you realize the damage you've done. Everything was going exactly as I planned, Captain. If you blue-boys and your scouts would have left me alone, right now we would be a giant step closer to solving the Indian trouble around here. As it is now, Keen Sighted now believes I set him up, and I don't blame him. The Apache understands deceit just like the white man." I hooked my thumb to the south. "Now you've set us back weeks, maybe even months." Trembling with anger, I paused, glaring at him.

He stared back with a murderous look in his close-set eyes. His blubbery cheeks were florid with anger. "I will remind you, Mr. Moore. I am commander of this district. My word is law. I can throw you in irons just as fast as I can anyone else, even if you do work for the government." His words were blustering, swaggering, those of a man trying to bluff his way through a bad situation.

I shook with anger. He had butchered the entire plan, and he knew it, but the fat-jowled blockhead would never admit it. I forced my voice to remain calm. "Look, Captain. You say your scouts reported a possible ambush. Fine. Then this foul-up is their fault, no one else's. Leave it at that, before anybody says anything he'll regret."

I took a step closer to him. My words were short and crisp, edged with a ragged anger. "I'm going to try to reach Keen Sighted again. This time, if I'm lucky to persuade him to even consider another meet-ing, I want you and this entire troop of blueboys to stay fifty miles away from me. You understand? Otherwise, I'm hauling my carcass back to Washington and dumping this entire fiasco at your feet.''

His ears burned with embarrassment. He did not move, but his eyes cut aside as a snicker came from one of the officers behind him. His rotund face reddened. ''Are you giving me an order, Mr. Moore?'' he demanded, his tone daring me to dispute him.

For a moment, I was tempted, but I couldn't afford to put myself in a position where I would be unable to help Keen Sighted, and that's exactly what would happen if I offended Simpson any further. He might decide to raise sand with Washington.

True, he could not discipline me, but he could arbitrarily withhold any assistance I might need, might even create a big enough flap to have me ordered back east. No, I had to choose my words carefully. Simpson could possibly throw up enough obstacles to prevent me from doing what I had to do. ''Captain, I am not giving you any orders. That is not my job. My job was to find Keen Sighted, determine his part with the renegades, and then report to my superiors so they can decide whether or not he should stand trial. Upon orders from them, I came to you for assistance.''

I wanted to add ''only when I ask for it,'' but discretion prevailed over frustration. Instead, I said, ''You are a busy man, with much on your mind trying to maintain discipline in this sector of Arizona Territory. In the future, I will only ask your help if it is absolutely essential to the success of our mission.'' I glanced at Big Bow, who wore an enigmatic smile on his dark face. I dismissed it. ''I do not wish to interfere with you or your troops.''

My response was out-and-out groveling, and I hated myself for doing it. Captain R. Albert Simpson was the dregs of the officer's corps. He had the integrity of a rattlesnake, the morals of a saloon girl, and a brain the size of a black-eyed pea. But for me to accomplish my job, to save my brother, I had to deal with this sad excuse for a human being by using any means possible short of two hundred and fifty grains of lead from the smoking barrel of a .45.

He snorted, still peeved at my earlier remarks. He glanced over his shoulder at his officers and gave them a smug grin.

I glanced at Lieutenant Irons, who was standing a step behind the captain. Irons cut his eyes from the captain to me and back again. When he saw me look at him, he dropped his gaze to the ground, refusing to look me in the eyes.

Captain Simpson took a deep breath, trying to pull his oversize belly up into his chest. His close-set eyes glittered with triumph. "I see we understand each other, Mr. Moore," he squeaked through the sneer on his fat lips.

More than anything in the world at that moment, I wanted to drive my fist between his eyes. But, with a terse nod, I replied, "We do, Captain."

He tried to hold my eyes, but he failed. He dropped his gaze and spun on his heel and barked out an order. "Mount the troops, Lieutenant."

I rode back to the bivouac area with the troop, my head throbbing. The wound was superficial. Hanging around by myself in the desert now was asking for trouble. The best idea was to return to camp, and then send out another message to Keen Sighted. Deep down, I recognized the futility of such a move. I knew with a sinking feeling that I would probably never receive an answer to any message I sent.

But I had to try.

During the ride, Captain Simpson dropped back beside me. "Have you decided what you are going to do now, Mr. Moore?" His question held a note of concern in it.

"Not yet. Get another message out, I guess."

"I'll send Big Bow to you. You can send him out again," he replied. "Perhaps you'll have better luck this time."

I glanced at him. He tried to appear genuinely concerned in helping, and if it had been anyone else, I would have believed them. But not Captain R. Albert Simpson. There was only one person he wanted to help, and that lucky man was not me. "Thanks, anyway, Captain, but I can't send Big Bow out again."

He frowned. "I don't understand. Why not?"

His total ignorance of Indians almost made me sick to my stomach. I answered his question very deliberately, carefully emphasizing each word. "Because, Captain Simpson, Keen Sighted will kill him on sight."

My words didn't seem to call up any real concern on the captain's part, so I continued. "He figures Big Bow was part of the trap. He won't wait for any explanation."

"Then how do you plan on talking to this Keen Sighted fellow yourself, Mr. Moore?"

For once, the fat captain had asked me a question I couldn't answer.

I shook my head. ''Beats me, Captain. Beats me.''
I turned my eyes back to the front.

He studied me a moment longer, then returned to
his place at the head of the column.

Heat rose in distorted waves across the sweltering
desert, exactly as they had on that day twenty-one
years earlier when I first saw Susan Leslie, the young
woman I knew as *Sons-ee-ah-ray*, Morning Star.

I had been hiding in a shrub of chaparral by the side
of a dusty trail when the bulky Conestoga jerked to a
halt. White dust billowed up around the legs of the
oxen and the wheels of the wagon. The tall lanky man
on the seat shaded his eyes against the sun and cocked
his head for a better look at me.

I huddled lower in the chaparral, peering through
the tangle of branches. A tiny girl's voice broke the
stillness of the sweltering head as she scooted around
on the seat by her father. ''Daddy? Boy. See boy.''

The man climbed down from the seat, a rifle in his
hand. He glanced around suspiciously, then turned
back to me. ''What are you doing out here, boy?''

Frightened, I cowered, clutching the big Bible to my
chest.

''What's wrong, Frank?'' a woman's voice asked.

''Looks like a lost boy, Martha.''

He picked his way around the cactus and chaparral.
''Come on out, son. There's nothing to be afraid of.''

I shook my head.

''Don't worry. I won't hurt you. I want to help.''
He held out his hand. ''You've been hurt,'' he added,
nodding to the side of my head.

I touched my finger to my head and felt a large knot

just above my temple. Dried blood crusted along my jaw.

"Come on, boy. Let the missus take a look at that. Then it looks like you could use some grub."

The genuine warmth and concern in his voice reminded me of someone, but I didn't know who. Suddenly, I couldn't hold back the tears. I stumbled from my hiding place and threw my arms around his waist, sobbing like a baby.

After a few minutes, he held me at arm's length. "What's your name, son?"

I opened my mouth to speak, then I frowned and looked at him in alarm. "I . . . I don't know. I can't remember. I can't remember my name."

John Leslie glanced at his wife and quickly placed a calming hand on my shoulder. "Easy, boy. Easy."

"Who is he, John?" called out the woman standing behind the the seat.

"A lost one, Martha. Young feller about ten, it appears. Needs some tendin'." He led me back to the wagon. "Climb on up, son. Hop in the back, and Mrs. Leslie will tend that knot on your head."

That evening as we sat around the fire, Susan snuggled in at my side. We had become friends during the afternoon, despite the six years' difference in our ages. Frank Leslie looked through my Bible. "Is this your folks' Bible?"

I shrugged. "I guess so. It was laying on the ground by me when I woke up."

Frank Leslie grunted and turned to the front of the Bible. He studied a page. "Humm, this says your ma and pa was Marcella and Lucius Moore, from Pennsylvania, but there ain't no mention of your name. Probably just hadn't writ it down yet.''

Mrs. Leslie grinned awkwardly. ''Lordy. I know the feeling. I ain't put little Susan's in our family book yet neither. I need to do that first chance.''

He closed the Bible and handed it back to me. ''Well, Mr. Moore, seeing as how everybody ought to have a given name, we need to find one for you, even though it will only be temporary until you get your memory back.'' He glanced at his wife. ''Almost like some kind of sign, Martha. Here we are, going to work at a mine at the bottom of a mountain named Ben Moore, and we got us a young feller needin' a given name.'' He looked at me. ''How does the handle Ben strike you, son? Ben Moore. A name from the past you can't remember, and one from the future that lays ahead of you.''

That seemed fine with me, almost fitting.

He went on to say, ''We've come here from Boonville, Missouri. I got myself a good job down at the copper mines at Santa Rita.'' He talked more about his family, hoping to make me feel more comfortable, and it must have worked, for I dozed off right in the middle of his talk.

I awoke in the middle of the night. I couldn't believe my ma and pa was gone, but for some reason I've never understood, I didn't hurt real bad. Maybe it was because I couldn't remember what they looked like, I couldn't picture their faces, so I couldn't miss them too much. Maybe they was like these fine folks that picked me up. Why, these folks could be my own for all I knew. They weren't, but you couldn't prove it by me. It was a strange and empty feeling.

I turned over and pulled the blanket over my head and cried myself to sleep, but that was the last time I ever cried. Next morning, I decided that I had been right lucky in being found by the Leslies, and I would make the best of it.

Two days later, they were dead, and Susan and me were strung over the haunches of a couple Indian ponies like tow sacks of corn.

A shout from the front of the cavalry column broke into my memories. Below us lay the bivouac. I decided then that I would ride into Tucson the next day.

That night, I groomed my roan carefully, making sure that he was sound. The last several days, he and I had covered a lot of desert, and tomorrow, I planned for us to cover more.

There were still questions that needed answering.

By the time the sun rose the next morning, I was ten miles from camp. I decided to ride straight through, stopping only to breathe the roan and quench our thirst.

We reached the adobe village of Tucson in late afternoon. By the time I stabled my horse and made myself presentable with a bath and clean clothes, it was nine o'clock, time for the cafe to close. I waited outside for Susan.

When she saw me, she stopped and glared.

I grinned. "Don't worry. I don't have him with me."

"I know," she said. "And you should be ashamed of yourself. I will never trust you again."

Chapter Six

Well, sir, you could have knocked me over with a willow branch. I shoved my slouch hat on the back of my head and stared down at her. "Now, what are you talking about?"

She jammed her fists in her hips and jutted her slender jaw at me. The dim light from the cafe window turned her green eyes black. "You know full well what I'm talking about. You tried to trap Keen Sighted."

Her accusation took the breath from me. I could only stare at her, tongue-tied. But, quickly, I realized just what had taken place since my meeting with Keen Sighted. Somehow, he had contacted her. That was the only way she could have possibly known of the fiasco in the desert. I wasn't certain of all of the implications of his visit to her, but if—

Susan interrupted my speculation. "Well, what do

60

you have to say for yourself?'' Her words were sharp and demanding.

Two dusty cowpokes sauntered from the cafe and paused when they heard the anger in her tone. I glanced at them. They eyed me suspiciously, for womenfolk in the West, whether waitresses or schoolmarms, were highly esteemed, and no self-respecting cowboy permitted another to treat them in any manner except with high regard.

I took her elbow. ''I'll explain while we walk.''

Fortunately for me, she allowed herself to be led down the boardwalk. The two cowpokes continued to watch. I ignored them as I explained exactly what had happened.

We halted in front of the parsonage. The stars bathed us with a cool bluish glow. I finally answered most of her questions to her satisfaction. But there were still some aspects of my mission that bothered her. ''How are you going to find him now?'' she asked. ''He won't trust you. Not after what happened.''

''I know.'' I dropped my hand to my holster and absently flipped the rawhide loop on and off the hammer of my .45. ''The only choice I have is to find him myself.''

Susan frowned. ''But, by now, word has spread about the ambush. Every Apache in Arizona Territory knows you're here after Keen Sighted.''

''That's right,'' I replied, trying to grin.

''They'll shoot you on sight.''

''I don't think so. I don't figure they'd want to give up the chance to enjoy a few days' torture.''

Susan's eyes grew wide, then narrowed. "And they will too."

I laughed, trying to convince myself as much as her. "It won't come to that. Even if they capture me, no one will dare do anything until they get word to Keen Sighted. They'll want him to get his own pleasure out of it." I paused. "That's where I have the advantage."

She laid her hand on my arm. "That's not much of an advantage."

The warmth of her fingers against my cold flesh filled me with a strange feeling. "Maybe not, but I've got to reach him. He's got to know what's happening, what the Army thinks is happening. He still rides with Standing Bear, and as long as he does, he's in trouble."

I hesitated and glanced over my shoulder into the darkness. Lowering my voice, I continued. "Keen Sighted might be as guilty as any of them. Maybe even more so, but he's my brother. If I can get him away from Standing Bear, perhaps Washington will go easy on him. Who knows, maybe if I tell them about our ranch, they'll let him go with me, and we'll all leave this godforsaken country."

She frowned at me. In the starlight, her eyes were hidden in dark pockets, but the puzzled frown on her was clearly discernible in the starlight. "Ranch? What ranch are you talking about?"

"I tried to tell you last time, but you wouldn't let me. I bought a small valley up in the Tetons of Wyoming. Wild game thick as bees on honey, grass so rich that you can grow a three-year-old steer in six months. I've got money put aside for stock and materials. I had planned on coming back and taking Keen Sighted with me. And now, you too,'' I added.

Her frown deepened. ''And now me? You didn't think about me at first?''

I shook my head and drew a deep breath. I didn't really understand just why she asked the question in the manner she did, like I had hurt her or something, but I didn't have time to puzzle out her feelings. ''Look, you and me have a lot of catching up to do, but, you've got to admit, last time, you didn't give me much of a chance to say anything.''

An embarrassed grin played over her lips. ''I'm sorry. You're right.'' She grabbed my hand. ''Come on in and meet the Beechers. We can talk to all hours, and you can sleep in the spare room.''

Before I could protest, she added, ''I don't care if you do have a room at the hotel. You're spending the night here, and that's final.''

I didn't argue. I felt good just being around Susan.

The Beechers were decent, honest people, the kind the West needed. A little gullible perhaps, blinded some by the white man's prejudices, deaf to what few champions the Apache did have, and insensitive to man's inhumanity to man, especially when the latter had red skin. But these were honest drawbacks for the Beechers, ones that would be rectified the longer they remained in the West and saw the truth for themselves.

Susan and I talked until three o'clock.

I told her how I had ventured back to Pennsylvania to the family of Lucius Moore, only to discover that Lucius and Marcella Moore were not my parents, that the Bible I had carried for years did not belong to me.

Tears welled in Susan's eyes. "Oh, Ben, I'm sorry."

"Don't be. I might never know my real name, but if Ben Moore is good enough for the white man, and A Long Way is good enough for the Apache, both names are good enough for me."

A becoming smile played over her face. "What's this about a ranch?"

I grimaced. "I bought one in Wyoming for Keen Sighted and me. I thought you were dead, that you . . ." I hesitated, realizing how abruptly I was going to drop the bad news on her.

I explained. "When Chato sent me away with the Bible eleven years ago, I stopped off in Boonville, Missouri. I remember your pa telling me that was where you all was from. I met your grandma and grandpa, and after I told them all that had happened, they said they was coming to get you." I paused.

Susan urged me to continue, her face aglow with anticipation. I hated to tell her the rest of the story, but she needed to know. "I figured they did come get you. After the war, I was back through Boonville, hoping to see you." I reached over and laid my big callused hand on hers. "The menfolk, your grandpa and uncles had been killed in the war. Your grandma was in an asylum. Her poor mind just snapped when she learned her husband and sons was all killed. Most of the people had moved away. No one knew about you. They figured that you was probably killed along with a lot of other civilians."

"But I couldn't believe that," I said. "They told me, but I didn't want to believe it. I just couldn't believe that pretty, little green-eyed blonde wasn't around any longer.'' I squeezed her hand. ''And I was right.''

Her eyes glistened with tears of happiness. I continued. ''So you see why I've got to get to Keen Sighted, to persuade him to go with us. The three of us together again, in the mountains of Wyoming. Just like when we were children up on the Mogollon Plateau or in the Cimarrons.'' My elation vanished momentarily as I thought of Chato and Broken Knee.

Susan read my thoughts. ''Yes,'' she whispered. ''They would have enjoyed it too.'' She looked into my eyes. ''Ben?''

''Yes.''

''Do you have to take him back to Washington?''

She was not being subtle. The white man and the Apache in me grappled with her question. I tried to explain. ''If he's guilty, and I don't, they'll send someone else. An important man was murdered. If we run, they'll follow, regardless of where we go. Our only hope is that we can show that Keen Sighted was not a leader of this renegade band, that he was not the one giving the orders. And even then, I'll have to call in every favor I have in Washington.''

She nodded, her face somber. ''Will that help?''

''I hope so, but I am not an important man.''

Her fingers tightened about my own. ''Then, why should you take the chance with his life?'' Her light green eyes darkened. She made a sweeping gesture to the south. ''Perhaps we should go now. We can journey to Mexico and then turn west to California and circle back to Wyoming. Only an Indian could follow a trail that random.''

She was right. Keen Sighted could lead us on such

a course through Mexico and California that no one, not even another Apache, could follow.

I wanted to do exactly what she suggested. I can't tell you how much I wanted to do it, but I couldn't. If I did, how could I live with John Cook's death? No. The only way to make a life for ourselves was by the law, as uncertain, as unpredictable, as unwieldy as it might be. Once Washington was satisfied, once Washington's thirst for justice was slaked, we were free.

I tried to explain my feelings to Susan, to help her understand just why I had to do it my way.

She sat back in the straight-back chair and folded her arms across her chest, drawing a soundproof barrier between us. The years with the Apache surfaced. "You cannot trust the white man. Don't you know that by now, *Ah-han-day*? He tells the Apache one thing, and does another."

"But we must live with ourselves, not the white man."

Her lips twisted in a wry grin. "Living among the whites has confused you. Where is the Apache boy I knew? The white man with whom I now speak is unknown to me."

Seething with frustration, I rode back to the bivouac. By the time I reached the foothills of the Tucsons, I had finally come to the conclusion that I would never convince that stubborn woman of anything she didn't want to be convinced of.

Chapter Seven

Just before sunrise next morning, I topped out on the mesa east of the bivouac. I reined in the roan and sat in my saddle staring down at the tented village below as it slowly came to life. My eyes burned from lack of sleep, and I had ridden a crick into my neck. My entire body ached from weariness. All I wanted to do was sleep, and forget.

Clicking my tongue and squeezing my knees against my horse's ribs, I urged the roan down the slope. I knew I would be able to sleep, but there was no way I could forget. Too much had happened, too much to those few people for whom I cared more than my own life.

The sharp, rich smell of woodsmoke mixed with the heavy aroma of boiling coffee drifted on the cool morning air. My stomach growled, and I figured that instead of stoking up my own fire, I'd beg a cup of Arizona mud from one of the enlisted men.

I wasn't particularly anxious to talk to either Simpson or Irons.

To my surprise, a small fire blazed in front of my tent. A blackened pot sat on the edge of the coals. A spider full of freshly baked sourdough sat beside the coals on the other side of the fire. A slab of venison sizzled in a skillet.

I stared down at the fire from my saddle, wondering if some jasper had just decided to take over my camp. Before I had a chance to consider it, a voice behind me broke into my thoughts. "Sit. Eat. Then we must talk."

I glanced over my shoulder. Big Bow stared up at me, his dark face inscrutable. Without another word, he squatted by the fire and turned the venison with the tip of his double-edged knife. He looked up at me impatiently.

Taking my time, I dismounted and tended to the roan. By the time I got back to the fire, the skillet sat on the edge of the fire by the coffeepot, and the sourdough had been cut into chunks in the spider, a cast-iron pot with three short legs.

Out of courtesy, I offered Big Bow a cup. With the impassive poise of the Apache, he nodded and accepted it. I heaped a tin plate with the grub and dug in. I remembered my manners when my mouth was full, so all I could do was nod and point like a baby at the spider and skillet.

Big Bow declined, instead sipping his coffee from the cup held in both hands as he watched me wolf down the venison. After the first half-dozen mouthfuls,

I slowed up, almost embarrassed at my display of gluttony.

As most Apaches, Big Bow wore a loincloth and deerskin boots. A tattered Army jacket, the brass buttons missing, hung from his wide shoulders. A broad headband of blue calico held his long black hair from his eyes. Unlike most Indians who scouted for the Federal Army, he did not appear to have lost any of his muscle tone, for wiry muscles rippled under his taut skin with each movement he made.

"Good," I mumbled, nodding at the grub.

He returned my nod, but remained silent, his black eyes trying to penetrate mine, trying to read my thoughts; but I refused to permit his to do so, keeping my own focused on the plate in my lap.

After I polished off all the grub in my plate, I poured another cup of coffee. I extended the pot to him, but he again declined.

Leaning back against my saddle, I removed my hat and sipped the coffee, enjoying its warmth on a full stomach. For a moment, I was with my brother back among the piñon and pine of the Mogollon Plateau. "*Gracias*."

"*De nada*."

We sat in silence for several minutes, neither of us looking at the other, but I couldn't help wondering why Big Bow had gone to so much trouble. So I asked him.

"At the beginning, I had bad feelings for you," he said. "I thought you to be like the brass buttons who care nothing for the Indian."

"Did I not tell you who I was, that I was brother to Keen Sighted?"

He shrugged, and for the first time, a faint grin curled his lips, sheepish, almost embarrassed. ''The white man calls himself our brother, and gives himself foolish names like Son-of-the-White-Father-in-the-Rising-Sun.'' His smile broadened.

His wry humor touched my own. I returned his grin. ''Or like Man-with-Mighty-Gun-that-Shoots-One-Thousand-Times-on-White-Horse-that-Gallops-Fast.''

He laughed, and I laughed with him at the white man's foolishness.

''Yes,'' he said when our laughter had died away. ''I see the Apache in you.'' He reached for the coffee and refilled his cup, a gesture not lost on me. He glanced at me, and I held mine out, and he filled it as I spoke.

''Though white, I share blood with Keen Sighted. I lived with him and Chato, his father, for ten summers before I left. Now I have returned to much unhappiness. Chato is with his fathers, and I want to take Keen Sighted from here, away from Arizona. I wish our lives to be as they were.''

Big Bow pondered my explanation. ''What you wish is good. That is the hope of all Apaches. But Keen Sighted will not go.''

I frowned. He had given voice to a fear of my own, one I had kept tucked away in the deepest recesses of my mind, one I had refused to even consider.

But now, this Indian scout was forcing me to face that fear. ''Why does Big Bow say so?''

He shrugged. ''This is his land. His struggle against the bluecoats sings of his refusal to give up what is his.''

Big Bow was right, but I hated to admit it. I

couldn't admit it. I had to keep trying. "Perhaps you are right, but I will see him again. And I will try to make him see that what I propose is good."

He nodded. "I, Big Bow, believe you are right. That is why I am here. I will help. I will go to Keen Sighted for you."

His offer surprised me. "Why would you do this for me?"

Big Bow poured the remainder of his coffee on the coals at the edge of the fire and rose to his feet. "I hear when you refuse the fat captain to send Big Bow to find Keen Sighted. That tells me that A Long Way is not as the other bluecoats. I tell myself that there is something different about this man who says he is brother to Keen Sighted, something the Apache understands. I will go for you."

I looked into his eyes and saw that we understood each other. "No. We ride together, tonight. Will the captain let you go?" I set the cup on the ground by my side.

Big Bow snorted and made a throw-away gesture toward the captain's tent. "I go where I wish. The captain is not a man. He is a coward. He is a liar." He jabbed his finger into his chest. "We saw no Apaches in the desert, only the three in the arroyo. Captain Simpson lies when he says we reported them."

I rose and offered him my hand. "I believe you."

He studied me a moment, then grunted. "Good." And he took my hand.

"Tonight," I said. "In the dark of the moon, we will meet at the large bend in the stream. Then we travel together to find my brother."

As Big Bow turned to leave, I remembered Black Wolf's remarks about the prospectors paying for blue-coat protection. I started to ask Big Bow of it, but decided to wait. There would be time later.

I slept off and on the remainder of the day and put myself around a solid meal that night, figuring on several days of short rations. Just before sundown, I rolled into my soogan and dropped into a deep slumber.

The next thing I knew, I was being shaken from my sleep by a wild-eyed young recruit. "Mr. Moore, Mr. Moore. The captain wants to see you right away."

Blinking away the sleep in my eyes, I sat up and stared around, momentarily confused. Instantly, however, I knew that our plan for tonight was impossible to carry out. Pulling on my moccasins, I slapped my hat on my head and, buckling on my .45, hurried to the captain's tent.

I pushed through the tent flaps. The yellow glow of the barn lantern struggled to illumine the interior of the tent, but shadows still lurked in the corners. Captain Simpson was fastening down his John Brown belt and sheathing his saber. He frowned at me. I guess he figured I should have knocked or something, but after Big Bow confirmed my suspicions about the ambush, I was in no mood to pussyfoot around about anything.

Lieutenant Irons stood in one corner like the meek housedog he was, and two armed citizens stood in the other corner. Another man, younger than the others, stood in the shadows of the third corner.

Captain Simpson spoke up, his voice heavy with sarcasm. "Well, Mr. Moore. I hope you'll be convinced now. Your Apache friend, Keen Sighted, and his band of renegades just murdered twelve people on

the Menoz Ranch northeast of Tucson.'' Before I
could say a word, he continued. ''Since you are so
anxious to *talk* to him, I figured you might like to
accompany us while we run the savages down and
hang them.''

A sick feeling hit me in the pit of the stomach, but
I did my best not to let Simpson know how his words
had affected me. ''How do you know it was Keen
Sighted?''

One of the citizens spoke up. ''I seen him, mister.
I've seen him before, and I shore enough recognized
that murderin' savage this time.'' His face was rigid
with anger, and his bony fist gripped the butt of his
revolver until his knuckles turned white. The other cit-
izen nodded.

''Where did they go?''

''East. Stayed in the foothills for a good piece before headin' up into the Santa Catalinas ten, twelve
miles down from town. Left a trail plain as day. We
won't have no trouble following them murdering
savages.''

I tried to suppress the grin that sprang unbidden to
my face, but I wasn't fast enough. Simpson caught it.
''And just what is so humorous about that, Mr.
Moore?''

The two men from Tucson glanced at Simpson, puzzled over his words, then turned angry eyes back at
me.

I shook my head. ''Let me ask you gentlemen one
more question, and then I'll answer the captain's.
What kind of trail did you say the renegades left?''

''Plain as day,'' replied one, looking at his friend
who nodded vigorous assent. ''Plain as day.''

His friend echoed the man's answer. "That's right. Plain as day."

"The Santa Catalinas, Captain," I explained, taking it slow and deliberate, just like I was trying to guide a child into putting on his first stocking, "were made for ambush. They are full of canyons and cul-de-sacs. If the trail is as clear as these gentlemen say, then the renegades are setting you up for a surprise party."

Simpson glared at me. "And you find that a laughing matter?" he asked, continuing to snipe at me.

I'm a patient man, but I had just about all of Captain R. Albert Simpson's petty tirades I could stomach. I studied him several seconds, deciding that this was one man whose assistance I could do without. "Death, Captain Simpson, is no laughing matter. To me, to your scouts, to any hombre who knows anything at all about the Apache, the reason for such a clear trail is obvious. He wants you to follow him. And you probably will, even knowing that you're riding into an ambush. Laughing, Captain? No. I smiled because I recognized the obvious intent of such a clear trail, and I assumed you did also. But I see I was mistaken."

The young man in the corner cleared his throat. I saw that he wore a handmade knife in a beaded sheath, obviously crafted by Indians. Navaho, maybe. I didn't recognize the circular design as anything Apache.

"Then, Mr. Moore, you may remain in camp."

"Forget it, Captain. I'm riding with you, whether you like it or not." I gestured to the citizens. "I don't want to see their bones bleaching in the sun." More than that, I wanted to be in a position where I could help Keen Sighted if he were with this band. I prayed that he wasn't, but I didn't think my prayers would help much for I just wasn't sure what kind of relationship I had with the good Lord. I hadn't been much on religion since I left the Apache.

The Tucson men looked at each other, then turned back to the captain. "Is he telling us the truth, Captain Simpson?"

Simpson nodded. "As he sees it, gentlemen. But rest assured. I will take a detachment large enough to handle any situation we might discover. A week from now, we will have the renegades under our control."

That seemed to satisfy them.

We were to pull out within the hour. At least, that's the command Captain Simpson gave his orderly.

I grumbled at the kink this new development tossed into my own plans. With me and Big Bow out there by ourselves, we had a chance to reach Keen Sighted; but now, with a troop of fifty men, we might as well kiss our chances good-bye.

Six hours later, at ten o'clock, just before Captain Simpson gave the order to move out, I rode to the head of the column and pulled up in front of him and the lieutenant. The younger man from back in the tent was with them. A look of frustration had darkened his face.

All three turned to face me when I pulled up. "Look, Captain. There's no love lost between us, but we're both working for the same thing, to stop all of this killing. I know this country. I'd be glad to ride out with your scouts." I nodded beyond the Tucsons. "The spot where the renegades probably went up into the Santa Catalinas is about forty miles or so to the east. Me and your scouts could get there and back by the time you make camp tonight. Maybe we can get a handle on where the Apache is hiding out.''

Captain Simpson stared at me with disdain. His reply was filled with arrogance. ''I neither solicit nor do I need your advice, Mr. Moore. I shall keep my scouts with me. I am more than capable of meeting any emergency we may face.'' He nodded to the rear of the column. ''If you insist on riding with us, please remain in the rear of the column.''

I stared at him. Which barrel did they scrape this ignoramus from? ''Gladly, Captain, gladly.'' Angrily I jerked the roan around and galloped to the rear.

Chapter Eight

A few moments later, the young man joined me. "Mind if I ride along with you, Mr. Moore?"

I threw him a brief glance. "Free country."

He pulled in beside me. He rode a long-haired mustang that looked like it had been running wild the week before. A short, solidly built young man, he was dressed in deerskin that fit snug over bulging biceps and thighs. He wore a black, stiff-brimmed hat with a rounded crown. Like me, he preferred moccasins. "Name's Rooney Catlett, out of Catletts Station in Virginia."

He grinned. His two front teeth were missing. He pulled off his hat and ran his stubby fingers through his black hair. "Shore gonna be hot today," he opined, just like he was talking to an old friend. "You'd figger them bluecoats would move about when it was nice an' cool, not in the middle of the day when the sun is frying buzzard eggs an' boiling creeks dry,'' he added, a broad grin splitting his square face. ''I figger somewhere along the way in their soldiering, each and ever' one of them officer soldiers musta got tied to a snubbing post and whupped on the head with with a singletree.''

I couldn't help being drawn to him. He was a likable sort, and I saw we shared common opinions about bluecoat officers. ''You sure you're not afraid to be seen with me?'' I asked, still angry with the captain.

''Hadn't thought much about it one way or 'nuther. I do what I'm told. Army hired me to scout, I scout. The man tells me to git, I git. Till then, I just prop my feet up and grin at the world.'' He spoke in an easygoing manner, just like he was announcing that he was going to lay down for an after-dinner snooze.

''Well, Rooney Catlett,'' I said, extending my hand. ''I'm right pleased to meet you.''

''Me too, Mr. Moore. To meet you, that is.''

''The name's Ben.'' I grinned.

He grinned back. ''Okay, Ben.''

The column moved out, due east into the blazing sun. Rooney Catlett was sure right about the mental capacities of the federal officers. Not even the dumbest of the good Lord's animals stays out in the middle of the day in Arizona except man.

Two hours later, my cotton shirt clung to my chest, soaked with sweat. The ripe, leathery smell of horse sweat rolled up from the lather on my roan's chest. Throughout the long day, we rode, a silent, heat-drained column skirting the foothills of the Tucson Mountains and snaking across the desert in muted lethargy, baking in the one-hundred-degree heat. The still air hung heavy on our shoulders, unstirred by the slightest breeze.

Just before sundown, we reached the foothills of the Catalinas. Rooney was ordered up to the captain. I laid a small fire and put on some coffee and fished out a handful of jerky from my saddlebags. When Rooney returned, I was stretched on my soogan, leaning against my saddle, sipping coffee and worrying on a stick of rawhide tough jerky.

"Going out?" I asked.

He nodded, glancing at the coffeepot and wrinkling his nose. "After it gits dark. Figgered I stop by an' let you know. Captain wants to know their position and strength."

I nodded to the pot. An empty cup sat on the ground by it. "Help yourself. Jerky's in the bags if you want some."

He grinned boyishly and wasted no time filling his cup and scooping up a handful of jerky. Squatting in front of me, he sipped the coffee and smacked his lips. "That's the way it oughta be brewed, black and thick, and hot as Old Scratch's pitchfork."

We ate in silence. I studied him, trying to guess his age. Twenty, I figured. "Catlett. That's not a too common name."

He laughed. "I growed up an orphan back in Virgina. I didn't have no last name, so I took the name of the village I grew up in."

I grinned, thinking of my own name. "Makes sense to me."

He returned my grin. A comfortable silence settled over us as we finished our coffee and rolled into our soogans. "Moon sets early. I reckon on sneaking a couple hours' sleep first.'' He pulled the blankets over his shoulders and turned his back to the small fire. Moments later, I heard the steady buzz of light snoring.

I allowed the fire to burn down and crawled into my own blankets earlier than usual, but I couldn't sleep. The back of my neck crawled. As a youth, I had often watched with fascination as the desert sidewinder buried itself in the sand, patiently awaiting its next unsuspecting victim. The renegades were playing the same game with us. Blundering blindly ahead, the entire column was being drawn into a trap, and the renegades were just sitting back, watching and waiting.

Just before eleven, Rooney Catlett rolled from his soogan and stretched the sleep from his blocky frame. I lay with my head cupped in my laced fingers, watching his shadowy figure silently. He slapped his hat on his head and stared down at me in the darkness. ''Better git some sleep, Mr. Moore. Otherwise, tomorrow's gonna be a mighty long day.''

I grinned. He didn't miss much, that boy. ''I told you before, the name's Ben. You be careful, hear?''

He gave me a short nod and disappeared into the night. Moments later, the ground vibrated softly with hoofbeats. I rolled over and pulled the blanket over my shoulders.

Hoofbeats awakened me well before dawn. By the time the returning scouts reached the bivouac, I was waiting beside the captain's tent for them. Rooney dismounted along with Big Bow and another Apache scout. He nodded at me. ''They're out there.''

''That's no surprise, is it?'' I replied, my tone implying that the Apache was toying with us like a bob-cat with a horned frog.

Before Rooney could reply, Lieutenant Irons appeared from out of nowhere, and Captain Simpson shoved the tent flaps aside and stepped outside. He threw me a disapproving glance before turning to his scouts. "Well, Mr. Catlett?"

Rooney hooked his thumb over his shoulder. "They're out there, Captain. Bedded down by a stream in a small valley. A few of 'em even threw up some wickiups." He hesitated, then added, "They're trying to make us think they're plannin' on spendin' some time there."

I looked at the captain for his response. He ignored me and asked, "Any women or children?" I don't know why, but his question surprised me, because it was one of the questions that needed to be asked.

"No papooses that I see'd. A couple women."

"You certain that's what they were?" I interrupted.

Captain Simpson glared at me. "I'll handle this, Mr. Moore. I believe I know the appropriate questions."

"Maybe you do, Captain, but did you know that often the Apache dresses his own men in skirts to fool people just like us?"

He glanced at Big Bow, who nodded agreement.

Chagrined, Simpson jerked his head around to face Catlett. "Could those women have been men?"

Rooney Catlett studied the question a moment. He arched an eyebrow and replied succinctly. "Yep."

Simpson glanced over his shoulder at Lieutenant Irons. The lanky officer shrugged.

"Well, Lieutenant, what do you think?"

Irons's Adam's apple bobbed in his skinny throat.

Nervously, he cut his eyes from Catlett to me, and then back to Captain Simpson. Indecision was scribbled across his thin face. He nodded hastily. "Same as you, sir. They have their squaws with them. The savages don't suspect a thing."

Captain Simpson's round face beamed with satisfaction. "That's how I figure it, Lieutenant." He waved a finger toward the Catalinas. "Lead the way, Mr. Rooney."

I couldn't sit back and watch a massacre explode before my eyes. "It's a trap, Captain. You take us in there, and any of us will be lucky to crawl out."

His brows knit in a deep V over the bridge of his nose, and his pig eyes turned cruel. "Then you remain behind, Mr. Moore. G Troop has no place for cowards in its ranks."

A blinding rage exploded in my brain, searing it with outrage. My hand flashed to the butt of my .45. I shook with fury. It was only with a tremendous amount of control that I was able to keep the Colt in the holster.

Simpson froze. From the corner of my eye, I saw the others were motionless also, caught by surprise.

My words struggled from my tight lips in a stranglehold. "You better thank that uniform, Simpson. That's the only thing that saved your life. But it won't do it twice." I paused, taking a deep breath as I struggled to control the fury boiling in my blood. "Next time . . ." I clenched my teeth, holding back the angry words battering at the back of my teeth.

"Watch it, Moore," said Lieutenant Irons, his deep voice breaking the tense silence.

I turned my silent fury on him. He parted his lips

to say more, but, thinking better of it, clamped them shut.

Turning back to Simpson, I said in a harsh whisper, "For your sake, there had better not be a next time."

He was shaken, but he tried to hide his fear beneath a transparent veil of belligerence. "You can't threaten me, Moore. I'll have—"

"I not only can, I did," I said, interrupting him. I hurled my next words in his fat, florid face. "And if you don't like it, then do something about it."

He said nothing. He just glared malevolently at me. I paid his stare no mind. "I'm telling you once again, Captain. This is a trap. If this is Standing Bear's bunch, you can bet your next year's pay he'll be waiting for you."

Simpson was not completely a fool. He turned to Rooney Catlett. "What do you think?"

Rooney scratched his head. "I wouldn't go rushing right in, Captain. I'd give it a little more time and watching."

The frown on Simpson's face told me all I needed to know. He did not believe me, and as soon as one of his scouts agreed with him, Simpson could justify giving the order to move out.

"What about you?" he asked of Big Bow, who had watched the entire proceedings without changing his expression from the weary, phlegmatic gaze he always wore.

The wiry Apache's eyes flicked at me, then focused on Captain Simpson. "If *ish-tia-nays* in camp, Apache do not expect trouble."

"*Ish-tia*-whats?"

Big Bow held his hand chest high, the palm facing the ground. "Women."

Simpson's face broke into a broad grin. He looked at me, gloating. "Give the orders to move out, Lieutentant," he said without taking his eyes from mine.

"Yes, sir."

I shook my head. "You're crazy, Captain. Crazy as a loon. There's no women in the camp."

He sneered. "That's not what my scouts report, Mr. Moore. Or have you now gone deaf?"

Chapter Nine

Ten minutes later, we moved out, heading deeper into the Catalinas, forbidding escarpments of granite that, except for the weather-rounded boulders, reminded me of the ominous Dragoon Mountains far to the east, the hideaway of Cochise.

Rooney rode back to me just before we pulled out. "Sorry, Ben. You heard. He wouldn't listen."

"I heard." And I knew Rooney would be riding point. "You watch out for yourself up there. It's been years since I saw Standing Bear. If anything, the years have made him smarter, and back when I knew him, he was the sneakiest Apache I've ever seen set up ambushes." I paused.

The blocky scout winked at me. "Don't worry none. I got me a mighty healthy respect for all them Apache."

"Good."

He grinned and headed back to the front of the column.

Slowly the rock-strewn slopes rose from the ground, shelving up into high serrated ridges, too steep to climb with any facility, but not too steep to provide an ideal ambush. We rode in the sandy wash between two steep slopes that twisted and turned and rose higher and deeper into the menacing mountains.

The sun baked us, driving the inexperienced soldier to his canteen too often. Sweat soaked our clothes, causing them to cling to our heat-wearied bodies. Our horses plodded, heads down, feet shuffling, too worn by the debilitating heat to even flick their tails at the nagging flies.

We stopped at noon. According to the scouts, the encampment was a half-mile ahead, nestled in the middle of a small valley between the two ridges on either side of us.

The order was given, and the metallic clanking of soldiers readying their weapons drifted across the silent troops in a subtle mutter. No one spoke. Men looked at each other, then glanced quickly away, hoping to hide the fear gnawing at their insides.

Leather creaked as men shifted in their saddles, inserting Springfield Trapdoors in boots. Fasteners snapped like click-bugs as holster flaps were unsnapped. Abruptly, without a word, all noise ceased. The troopers sat tall in their saddles, faces pale and drawn, but jaws clenched and eyes cold.

I had to admit, while I figured we were all loco as an Apache on rotgut whiskey to be blundering ahead as we were, these young troopers struck me as gutsy fellers I could be proud to go to the well with.

The sand silenced the hooves of the cavalry horses. Only the rhythmic creak-creak of the saddles disturbed the silence of blistering air. Within minutes, the troop halted near the crest of a ridge. I looked at Simpson, who balanced on his tired horse and peered down into the valley at the small cluster of wickiups.

Beyond him in the camp that straddled the small stream, two or three Indians strolled idly, oblivious to our presence, another indication that they were laying for us. Indians, especially Apache, have a sixth sense about white men.

I looked into the heights of the ridges far above the valley. The slopes of the ridges were dotted with boulders and rifts in the granite, affording ideal hiding places for an ambush. That was exactly where I would be if I had been in Standing Bear's shoes.

Muttering dark oaths, I started to heel my roan back to the front of the column, but I was too late. Simpson yelled at the bugler, who immediately blasted out the vibrant, rapid notes of the charge. As one, the troop leaped forward, sabers flashing, rifles drawn, arches firm in the stirrups, and legs extended. Adrenaline-charged bodies leaned forward over the necks of their horses.

A wild surge of excitement plastered a grim smile across their faces, one that would last until the first impact, then would dissolve with the sudden realization that they rode side by side with death.

The three Apaches didn't even look at us. With the first note of the bugle, they ripped off their dresses and dashed into the willow brakes above the camp. Seconds later, three ponies burst from the willows and raced to the far end of the canyon.

With a yell of triumph, Simpson spurred his horse after the retreating Apaches. Exactly what they wanted him to do. I yelled, but my voice was lost in the confusion.

Without warning, the nearest Apache jumped from his pony and turned to face us, a rifle in his hand. He kicked off his moccasins and planted his bare feet on the ground. His gray hair fell about his shoulders.

Our troop slowed. I tried to scream out a warning when I saw him kick off his moccasins, but the sounds of his gunfire, and the resulting gunfire from our troop drowned my words. He jerked his rifle into his shoulder and fired. A trooper screamed and tumbled backward out of his saddle.

As one, G Troop pulled up and fired at the single Apache, then spurred their animals forward once again.

The single Apache staggered, but remained on his feet, his body riddled with slugs as we bore down on him. He continued firing, until a slug caught him in the middle of the forehead and knocked him backward. Simpson's harsh voice carried above the tumult, and he drove his horse onward in continued pursuit of the remaining two Apaches. Suddenly, the slopes of the ridges exploded with gunfire and arrows.

The trooper in front of me screamed and flung out his arms and tumbled backward out of his saddle. Another yelled and grabbed at the arrow that suddenly appeared in his chest. A trickle of blood ran down the side of his lips, and then I swept past him, my .45 in hand, leaning low over my saddle as I followed the troop.

I had no choice. I wouldn't last any longer than the

proverbial snowball if I broke away. I had to stay with
G Troop, and the slaughter that lay ahead.

Suddenly, the troop was doubling back on me, led
by Simpson, whose fat face glistened with fear. ''The
willows,'' I yelled, waving the muzzle of my revolver
at them. ''Set up a perimeter around the willows.''

He stared at me unseeing. I yelled again. My words
registered this time, and he angled toward the willow
brake, bouncing in the saddle like a green recruit.

The gunfire was murderous, unrelenting, a storm of
slugs and arrows so thick that if you were agile and
fast enough, you could've walked out of the valley on
them. Less than half of us made the willows. We dismounted on the run, diving for the nearest cover. Our
horses, frightened by the incessant rifle fire, bolted.
Probably right into the hands of half a dozen waiting
Apaches who would herd them back to their own
remuda.

Once in the brake, our casualties diminished, for
while the willows did not stop the slugs, they did hide
us from the Apache. He was shooting blind now, but
from time to time, it paid off as a soldier jumped to
his feet and screamed.

The initial intensity of the Apache fire lessened as
the afternoon dragged by. Rooney and I had wormed
out a small depression underneath a windfall where
we gained slight protection against the random slugs.

I glanced at the sun balancing on one of the mountain peaks. ''We're pinned here till dark. That's when
we've got to make a break for it.''

''We're gonna try to break out of here?'' His voice
was incredulous. ''We got no horses.''

''You got a better offer?''

He took a deep breath and stared through the willows at the slopes above us. "I don't reckon so."

"Then that's what we do come night."

We lapsed into silence as occasional slugs whined overhead or whumped into the sand at our feet. For several moments, no slugs came near us. A sharp command echoed down from the slopes, and an explosion of gunfire followed. At first I figured the Apache had tired of his game with us, but then I recognized the new strategy Standing Bear had employed. I closed my eyes and shook my head. We were in one mighty bad spot.

The gunfire was now measured and deliberate, not the ragged gunfire of thirty individuals, but the fire of thirty focused weapons. Following each shout, which was their signal, the slopes exploded with gunfire.

Cries to "dig in" came from up and down the line. Soldiers screamed. A few old hands tried to calm them, but the truth was, Standing Bear had us exactly where he wanted us. In ten minutes, unless we took quick action, most of us would be lying facedown in the sand, our blood mixing with the muddy water of the small stream curving through the brake.

The sun dropped behind the mountains, filling the bowl of the valley with shadows. If we could hold out another thirty minutes . . .

I peered over the windfall. The scathing gunfire was being concentrated on the downstream section of our hastily erected bulwarks. A trooper screamed, then another. Beneath the racketing of gunfire, the piteous moans of the wounded drifted down to us. Gunsmoke stung our eyes.

"Blast!" I exclaimed.

Rooney looked around at me.

I nodded downstream. "I wondered when they would try it," I muttered.

The young scout gave me a baffled look.

I explained, speaking loudly to be heard over the firing. "They're coordinating their fire. They're moving toward us."

"I don't follow you."

Quickly I drew a line in the sand. At one end of the line, I drew a small box. "Here's where they're concentrating their fire now." I drew another box adjacent to the first. "Then they'll concentrate their fire on this area." I drew several more boxes along the line. "After completely wiping out everything in this spot, they'll move their fire a few feet, and concentrate on this next sector. They'll move slowly along our barricade, saturating one area of our defense before moving to the next. Until . . ." I jabbed my finger in the last box on the line. "Until they reach us, right here."

He shook his head in wonder. "That's just like regular Army."

Despite the impending assault on our position, I couldn't resist grinning. Rooney Catlett was beginning to grow up about the Apache. I just hope he lived to learn some more. "They wrote the book," I said.

He sat back, staring at the lines in the sand, but I had already started making preparations. "What do we do?" he asked.

I gestured to the depression beneath the ancient oak under which we had taken shelter. "We dig out about a foot of sand and stick our behinds as far under this log as we can and hope that's deep enough."

We clawed at the sand with our fingers, dumping it

on top of the windfall for additional shelter. Another trooper's scream echoed above the steady firing as we completed our task and curled up back under the log. A few minutes later, Rooney yelled above the racket. "Why'd he do it?"

We had to shout to be heard. "Who?" I frowned at him, thinking he was referring to the captain. "Simpson?"

"No. That Apache. The one that jumped down and faced off with us. Didn't he know it was suicide?"

I glanced behind us. The gunfire was coming closer. I'd seen a lot more convenient times to carry on a conversation, but somehow, not one that was any better. "He was an old man. He wanted to die."

The frown on his face deepened. "I've heard of that before, but I never believed it."

Despite the battle raging about us, his words brought back memories that flooded through my head. For a brief few moments, the battle ceased to exist. Time was suspended, and I stood alone in my own world looking down on the only family I had ever known. "The Apache believes he is dead when he is no longer young. The young men fight and raid, which is the life of the Apache. To him, a fortune built on theft is to be admired just as we admire a man who builds a railroad. That's why the Apache can't understand why the white man gets so upset when he steals a few horses or cows from us."

Rooney nodded. "But what about that old man?"

"Every Apache hopes that he dies in battle. You saw him kick off his moccasins, didn't you?"

A fresh burst of gunfire caused us both to look around. Our turn was fast coming.

"Yeah. I wondered about that," he shouted. "What did that mean?" he asked, eager, as were most natural-born scouts, for a new insight into the mind or perspective of those with whom he must deal.

"That was his way of saying, 'I move no more.' "

He pondered my explanation a moment, then muttered, "Makes a man stop and think, don't it?" He hesitated and gestured to the bullet-riddled area around us. " 'Course, this makes a jasper stop and think too."

I looked at the young scout before me, but I saw in his face that of Chato's, and Colored Beads, and many others who now had long been with their fathers and their fathers' fathers in the world beyond. These men lived by the same credo as that old Apache lying dead not a hundred yards from us. Perhaps, Chato and those who preceded him were right. Old age is death.

One part of me felt as they. But another part said no.

I ducked as a slug tore out a chunk of oak just above my head. Rooney looked at me, his eyes wide with fear. I swallowed at my own fear clogging my throat. "Now I wish we'd dug this hole clean down to China."

He forced a weak grin. "Me too."

We both huddled as far back under that log as we could.

Suddenly, the sand around us erupted in dozens of small geysers of sand, slugs smashed and tore at the log above us, arrows stabbed into the ground, their shafts vibrating with the impact.

Like gusts of rain racing across a field in sweeping patterns, the slugs left their footsteps as they traced their way across the sand in military precision, methodically ripping apart everything within their fifteen-foot-wide sweep. Then the firing ceased, moved over fifteen feet, and began its journey back.

With mixed feelings, I shook my head in wonder at the capabilities of my Apache family.

"I figured you was right," Rooney said, changing the subject on me.

"About what?" I continued to watch the progess of the slugs, just in case they headed back in our direction.

"The ambush. How'd you know?

The sun had slid lower, darkening the shadows pooling in the valley. A few more minutes, I figured. The gunfire slowed. Come dark, the firing would cease, but the security would tighten. They wanted to keep us inside the valley until morning when they could finish the job.

"Well?"

"I grew up Apache. Those men up there," I said, nodding toward the slopes, "they're men I grew up with."

The small cave in which we huddled was too dark to discern features, but I knew Rooney Catlett was staring at me in surprise.

I ignored him. Sticking my head from under the windfall, I peered over the earthworks we had thrown up, but I had no idea how many of us still lived. I turned back to Rooney. "Now listen. I grew up around here. There's a way out, but you're going to have to make Simpson believe it's your idea. The man is so mule-stubborn that if he thought I was behind it, he would balk and get every last one of these men killed. You understand?"

Rooney gulped. "Yeah," he whispered.

"Okay. Now look." I pointed to the southeast where the darkness hung heavy along the edge of the valley. "Over there is a patch of cedar. Behind the cedar is a narrow canyon that winds its way back to the desert. Give me twenty minutes. Then you just lead these soldier boys to it. That's all."

"What if I can't find it?"

"You will. There's only one patch of cedars. You can't miss it." It was dark now, so dark our faces were blurred outlines even though we were only inches apart, but I could sense Rooney wasn't convinced by what I said. "Once you're out of these willows, you'll be able to see a little from the starlight. I'll lay two branches on the sand to mark the entrance to the trail through the cedars. Go straight through the brake, and you can't miss the canyon."

"Okay," Rooney replied. "Those branches. Like an 'X' or something?"

"No. Apache sees them, he knows something's out of kilter. Nature doesn't go around dropping branches in the shape of an 'X'. I'll lay them so one is touching the other at one end. Now, once you get in the canyon, keep going, no matter what you hear. It comes out by a spring with good cover. Then all you got to worry about is a twenty-mile hike back to Tucson, due west." I glanced at the stars. They sparkled against the black velvet of the night, so many, so thick they seemed to be rubbing shoulders. "And you got a good night for it."

"What about you?"

"I got plans to keep these Apache boys busy. Remember, twenty minutes."

That satisfied Rooney, and he disappeared into the darkness toward Captain Simpson's bulwark. I slung a canteen over my shoulder.

After marking the entrance to the narrow canyon, I slipped silently up the mountain, hoping to discover where they had staked out their ponies. If I could spook their mounts, they would be forced to give up their assault on the troop.

Once, when I was younger and in practice, I could have slipped in among a roomful of wild hogs without being spotted, but that was before I went to live with the white man. Now, I wondered.

Chapter Ten

I located the Indian ponies grazing on scrub in a hollow buried back in one of the rocky canyons far north of the trail I told Rooney to use. I had to move quickly, and quietly. My twenty minutes were running out. I knew there would be at least one, possibly two sentries with the ponies.

Staying behind the boulders, I eased around the hollow, which was about an acre in size. The whisper of a moccasin on granite broke the stillness. I slipped into the shadows of a boulder as the footsteps came my way. I palmed my Colt and crouched lower, holding my breath. When the guard passed, I struck him across his temple. He folded to the ground without a murmur. I dropped back into the shadows, my revolver ready in case someone gave an alarm. But the night remained silent.

Quickly I pulled the sentry into the shadows beside

the faint trail, whipped off his deerskin vest, and slipped it on. With ever increasing confidence in my own stealth, I eased around the perimeter of the hollow. The ponies snuffled and stirred uneasily at the smell of a white man, but the smell was subdued by the vest I had taken from the sentry. The ponies continued grazing. I found no one else. The single Apache was the only guard.

Now was not the time for silence. I fired into the night and ran shouting into the herd of ponies, waving the vest over my head. As one, they bolted. Hooves clattered on granite. Strained grunts and frightened squeals broke the silence as the animals flashed through the night and disappeared down the mountain.

I found a small niche between two boulders back off the track and slipped inside. Moments later, the pounding of moccasined feet raced down the path in pursuit of the ponies.

Even after the last footsteps had faded into the darkness, I remained hidden. There was no hurry. Once Rooney and the troops reached the spring, they were safe.

But in my satisfaction at having broken up the ambush, I grew careless. The Apache has infinite patience. An *ish-kay-nay* often lies on the ground by the hole of a ground squirrel or chipmunk for hours, looped snare in hand, waiting for the tiny animal to stick its head out. And that young boy carries that same patience with him into his manhood. This time, they were waiting for me; instead of a looped snare, they had guns.

I left the boulders too soon, for just as my moccasins touched the granite outside my hideout, the click of a cocking hammer broke the still mountain air. I threw myself sideways, shucking my own six-gun as a gun roared and a flash of yellow lit the darkness. A slug whistled past. I hit the ground and tossed a shot behind me. Bouncing to my feet, I scrabbled back into the rocks, clambering my way up a short slope, and hoping I wasn't running into a dead end.

More gunfire erupted behind me. Slugs whined off the rocks, none close, for the Apaches were firing at shadows. I paused to grab a handful of rocks. I lobbed one off to my left and made another dash up the slope. Behind me, flashes of light burst in the night as the Apaches fired at the noise made by the clattering rock. I threw another stone and eased over the crest of the slope.

A guttural voice rose above the gunfire, which immediately ceased. Grimly, I realized they had tumbled to my ruse. I tossed one more rock, but its banging and clattering elicited no further gunfire.

Quickly I made my way down the slope, keeping my ears cocked for any pursuit. Once or twice, I heard the murmur of a foot sliding on granite behind me. At the base of the slope, I cut west, doubling back to the willows.

Before reaching the valley, I slipped through a tangle of mesquite and brittlebush and hid behind a boulder several feet away. Sure enough, minutes later, a dark shadow paused to inspect the mesquite, then continued on to the valley.

I waited an hour, then headed due south, scaling another ridge, and then another. At the crest of the second ridge, I found a fissure about three feet high and five feet deep in a granite wall. I slipped inside

and stacked small boulders in the entrance. Unsheath-
ing my knife just in case a rattlesnake wanted to share
my bed, I leaned back in my cramped quarters and
waited for daylight.

Despite impending dangers or anticipated dreams, a
man's body must rest. When muscles tire, and the
brain wearies, and senses numb, the body shuts down
and recharges itself. An infant falls asleep on the floor
in the middle of his toys, a youth on the bank of his
fishing hole, and a man in the saddle.

After the sounds of pursuit faded outside my cave,
I relaxed. Moments later, I slept. I awakened with a
start. Listening carefully, however, I heard nothing. I
sipped at the canteen. The warm water was more welcome than a mug of beer after a long afternoon splitting rails.

I removed a few small rocks from the opening so I
could keep an eye on the slope beneath me. Only the
gentle soughing of the warming breeze working its
way up the mountainside broke the silence. I leaned
back and waited, my eyes scanning the rocky slope
before me, my ears cocked for any sound other than
that of the soft wind. I would not again permit myself
to forget the patience of the Apache. I had departed
my hideout the night before too soon and almost ended
up with my skin punched full of holes in all the wrong
places. That was a mistake I would not make again.

Sometime later, a couple of ground squirrels skit-
tered around playfully in front of the fissure. They
were disturbed when a rabbit appeared. With angry
chattering, they hopped up on a small boulder and
fussed at the cottontail. Later, after the squirrels and
rabbit disappeared, a pair of gray doves fluttered down

and scratched up a meal from the sand deposited in the rifts in the granite. I grinned to myself. The Apache in me told me I was alone on the mountainside. It was time to go.

I slipped from the fissure and stretched the kinks out of my muscles. In the distance, the squat, shabby village of Tucson appeared distorted in the rising heat waves.

The troops should be there by now, I guessed.

Staying under cover as much as possible, I wound my way down the mountain and into the foothills, which were thickly dotted with shiny green mesquite, spindly spires of soapweed yucca, jumping cholla, and majestic saguaro. I found a small nook in the shade of a patch of young mesquite and after making sure no snakes were taking advantage of the cool shade, crawled inside to await the night. I much preferred the dangers of night travel through the foothills and across the desert than those of the day.

Late that afternoon, I spied a spiral of smoke from a mountain peak just beyond the valley in which we were ambushed. The thin column of unbroken smoke rose steadily, telling me, and those for whose eyes it was intended, all we needed to know. The maker of the smoke was calling his people together.

I smiled grimly, feeling my parched lips crack. That signal would be bringing in Apaches from twenty miles around. If I'd been out on the desert, they would have discovered me without fail.

Slowly the sun rolled down the western sky. I had about four hours of darkness between the time the sun set and the moon rose. I stretched my legs as best I could under the mesquite, wanting to waste no time once I started.

With dusk came the nightly rebirth of the desert. Rodents scampered. Owls swooped. Rattlesnakes searched.

I picked my way out of the foothills while I could still see to place my feet. An upset rattlesnake was not my idea of a new type of sole for my moccasin.

By the time I left the foothills, the stars lit the desert with an eerie blue glow. Quickly I dropped into a steady trot. As an Apache youth, I had grown up with twenty-mile runs, on occasion, without a drop of water. Now I felt the reassuring pressure of the canteen against my hip.

I reached Tucson around four o'clock. Susan and the Beechers put me up for a couple hours' sleep, but not before she wormed out everything that had happened since I had last seen her.

The parson and his wife had gone back to bed, and Susan and I sat around the kitchen table sipping coffee. "But you are going back to help Keen Sighted, aren't you?" she asked.

"As soon as I can. That's the only reason I went with the army on this patrol. He was supposed to be with that band. I wanted to be there to help him."

"But you didn't see him?"

"Not a trace. But if he was there, he sure saw us," I replied, unable to resist grinning at the irony of the situation.

"So, now what?"

I explained to her how Big Bow and I had planned to go into the desert after him. Not much of a plan, I admitted, but I was open for suggestions.

"But, if he thinks you betrayed him once, what makes you believe he'll trust you this time?"

That was a question I had asked myself, and one for which I had no answer. "I've just got to try."

She smiled at me sadly and laid her hand on mine. "I'll pray for you both."

The touch of her hand on mine sent shivers up my spine. I'd never noticed it before, but around Susan, I felt almost . . . well, almost like a whole person, complete, satisfied. I wondered if she felt the same around me. "I don't know about Keen Sighted," I replied lightly. "But speaking for myself, I can use all the help you can give me."

I should have noticed the funny look Susan got on her face, but I didn't. I was worn to a nub, like a worn-out chopping hoe.

After our visit, I slept for a couple hours, borrowed a pony and gear from the hostler with the help of the parson, and headed to the bivouac area. The day was hot, and the ride was lonely. The pony was a blood bay, and she fox-trotted along real nice and smooth, which was unusual for a cow pony. Maybe there was something in having a preacher on your side.

I noticed the odd looks given me when I reached camp, but dismissed them as being nothing other than simple curiosity. Dismounting in front of my own tent, I began to unsaddle the borrowed pony. Later, I would check the remuda to see if by any chance my roan had made it back.

Suddenly, two soldiers appeared, each bearing his Springfield at port arms. "My respects, Mr. Moore. Captain Simpson has sent us to bring you to headquarters."

I pulled the saddle from the pony and dropped it by my tent. "Be right there, Private. Soon as I finish here."

"Sorry, sir. He said immediately."

The tone of the private's voice made me look around. He gulped and nodded. "That's what he said, sir. Right now." His face was pale with nervousness, but his jaw was set.

I fastened the reins to the saddle. "Lead on, Private."

He relaxed noticeably, and a faint grin replaced the grimness on his face. "Thank you, sir."

Simpson was waiting for me along with Lieutenant William J. Irons, Rooney Catlett, and Sheriff Samuel Black. "Here he is, Sheriff," said Simpson when I entered. He pointed his finger at me. "Here's the traitor that led us into that ambush. I demand you arrest him."

Immediately, I realized what Simpson was up to. Shift the blame. Make me the scapegoat. Well, thanks, but no thanks. I jumped back, my hand leaping for my revolver, but I froze when I felt the cold muzzles of two Springfields in my back. I looked at the sheriff. "He's lying, Sheriff. I tried to stop him."

Rooney Catlett sidled back into a corner, his gaze flicking from Simpson to the sheriff, then to me.

Lieutenant Irons spoke up. "Moore's the one who's lying now, Sheriff." I looked at Irons in surprise. That was probably the longest speech I had ever heard him make. He continued, his voice shaking with nervousness. "Both the captain and I argued with him, but he insisted there was no danger." He paused, then added, "We're not experts on the Apache like you or the other westerners are, Sheriff Black. We're forced to listen and act upon the advice of those around us.''

I shook my head. ''It's hard to believe a great man like General James Irons could have a grandson like you, Lieutenant. From all I ever heard about that fine old gentleman, he never told a lie in his life. But I reckon you're doing your best to make up for it.'' I glanced at Rooney Catlett, but he remained in his corner, his eyes still darting from one to the other. It appeared he was having trouble picking his side.

The sheriff sucked in his melon-size belly and nodded, completely suckered by the lieutenant's whining. ''Yore dadburned tootin' right about that, Lieutenant.'' He let fly a stream of tobacco juice on the ground at his feet to punctuate his response.

''That's why I asked you to come out here, Sheriff,'' put in Simpson. ''Moore here is not military. He's a civilian, and you can arrest him for treason.''

Sheriff Black glared at me ''I reckon I can sure do that.'' For a fleeting moment, I thought I saw a look of triumph in his black eyes.

Just as the sheriff reached for his revolver, Rooney Catlett made up his mind and stepped forward. ''That ain't exactly the truth, Sheriff.''

Simpson stiffened, and Irons's mouth dropped open. ''Mr. Catlett,'' snapped Captain Simpson. ''You have no business here. You are dismissed.''

Rooney looked at him, gathered a wad of saliva, and squirted it on the dirt floor at the sheriff's feet. He shot a brief, withering look at Irons, and then said, ''I reckon not, Captain. I reckon I just quit the Army. One spineless jasper in a troop is enough.'' He kept his eyes fastened on Simpson. ''What you two told

Sheriff Black here is a lie bigger'n Texas. I heard Ben try to talk you out of the patrol, but you wouldn't listen.''

The muscular young scout paused and turned to the sheriff, who wiped the back of his hand over his lips and shot a nervous glance at Simpson. ''I don't know what all is takin' place, Sheriff, but you ask any of the scouts, and they'll tell you what I say is true.''

Black looked back at Simpson awkwardly, and from the confused expression on his face, I realized that the entire plot had been set up, that the sheriff was as much a part of the farce as the captain. He stammered for words to save his face. ''Well, it . . . huh, well, Captain. It seems like there is some kind of disagreement here. Maybe, you . . . uh, oughta—''

''Rethink, Sheriff. Is that the word you're looking for?'' I asked, glaring at the man.

He nodded gratefully. ''Yeah. That's it. Maybe we . . . I mean . . . you and Captain Simpson, might oughta . . .''

I stared hard at Simpson. His watery green eyes wavered, then turned cold when they recognized the disgust mine held for him. ''That's a smart idea, Sheriff Black,'' I said in a hiss. I wanted to say more, but I held my tongue. My time would come. I turned and pushed past the two guards and left the tent while the sheriff was still trying to form a sentence. Rooney tagged after me.

Outside, I gave him a wry grin. ''Looks to me like you just tossed a long and lustrous career with the Army in the river.''

He grinned crookedly. ''It do, don't it? 'Course,''

he added, somewhat sheepishly, "it took me a few minutes to decide about doing it. Sorry."

"Forget it. Man should look after his skin first."

"Up to a point," Rooney replied.

I grinned.

Twenty minutes later, the sheriff rode out of camp. "From what I hear about that jasper," Rooney said, "he's gonna be a rich man."

"How's that?"

The young man shrugged. "What Big Bow says is that he's the middle man between the bluecoats and prospectors. Somehow, he arranges for gold hunters to come in and prospect under the protection of the Army."

I remembered the conversation my first morning on the river bank with Strong Swimmer and Black Wolf. So they had been right. Someone was stealing Apache gold. No wonder the Indian was so angry and suspicious. I wished I could have done something to help them, but my hands were full at the present.

That night, Rooney, Big Bow, and I squatted around my fire and talked softly of our next step. I couldn't help thinking as I looked at them over the small flames licking at the bottom of the coffeepot that here were two men I wouldn't mind riding the river with, two that I could count on.

"Now what, Ben?" Rooney rose and poured another cup of coffee.

Big Bow's thin lips parted in a grin when I replied. "I reckon I'll mosey out there and do a little palavering with Keen Sighted."

The Apache scout shook his head. "You can grab water with your fingers easier."

Before I could reply to his wry remark, the beat of a galloping horse echoed through the night. It came from the direction of Tucson. I looked in the direction of the hoofbeats. The horse slid to a stop in front of the captain's tent, and the rider leaped to the ground as the captain rushed outside.

I couldn't make out what they were saying, but the rider's frantic gestures indicated that there was serious trouble in Tucson. I looked back at Rooney and Big Bow. The Apache had disappeared.

Captain Simpson's voice rose above the tumult. "Lieutenant. Mount a patrol." I saw a shadow rise from the ground by the side of the tent. Big Bow! The captain turned back to the messenger and spoke rapidly. The messenger nodded and pointed north. With a curt nod, Captain Simpson hurried back into his tent, and Big Bow faded into the ground.

Moments later, the Apache scout suddenly appeared at my campfire. His face was somber.

"What is it?" I asked.

"White woman. From Tucson. They say she was taken by Apaches."

"And Simpson's going after her?"

"Yes," he replied, his black eyes boring into mine.

A sense of uneasiness crept over me as Big Bow continued to stare at me. "What's wrong?" I asked.

"The night you came to Tucson, I see you on street."

I shook my head. "I don't . . ." Then I remembered. "Okay. You were with a patrol of troopers. I remember now."

He nodded. "And the woman with whom you spoke . . ." Big Bow paused.

I prompted him. "What about her?"

"She is the one of which they speak. She is the one taken by the Apache."

Chapter Eleven

For a moment, his words failed to register. He couldn't be talking about Susan. I stared at him in disbelief, a flame of anger igniting inside me. I felt another thin veneer of the white man slip away as the Apache desire for revenge began to boil.

Rooney Catlett spoke up. "Are you right sure you heard them plain, Big Bow?"

I knew he had, and an icy resolve settled over me, froze the unpredictable anger seething in my blood. I figured she was alive, that whoever had taken her had no plans to kill her, at least, not right away. I had to move, and fast. And I didn't have time to sort the mixed emotions racing through my body.

The Apache nodded, his face unreadable as he replied to Rooney's question. "I hear good. The white woman and two men leave Tucson for the mountains to the east."

To search for Keen Sighted, I told myself. ''Go on.''

''The men were found dead, scalped where the mountain trail forks to Fort Bowie.'' He stared hard at me when he said the word *scalped*. Then he continued. ''The law in Tucson says they were Apache.''

Rooney slammed a fist into the palm of his hand. ''Blast them devils,'' he hissed.

I looked at Big Bow, who arched a skeptical eyebrow at the young white scout. I understood exactly what Big Bow hinted when he stressed the word *scalped*. ''Apaches didn't take her, Rooney,'' I said.

He looked up at me in surprise. ''What do you mean?''

''I mean, it was probably Comanche. Maybe Paiute, but I don't really reckon so. Most likely, it was Comanche.''

Big Bow nodded his agreement.

Rooney frowned. ''How come you're so certain?''

''I'm not, at least whether it was Comanche or Paiute, but I'm dead certain it wasn't Apache.''

Rooney glanced at Big Bow who nodded, then looked back at me. ''Why?''

''Apache don't scalp.''

He looked at me in disbelief. ''They don't what?''

Big Bow grunted. ''He speaks true. The Apache only takes Mexican scalps. Never the white man.''

The muscular scout looked askance from Big Bow to me. I nodded. ''Years back, the Mexicans put bounties on Apache scalps, braves, women, and even the children. The Apaches are just repaying a debt, but never have they lifted a white man's scalp.

And this time is no exception.'' I pressed my fingers

against my forehead and dragged them slowly down my face. I was exhausted, but there was no time for rest.

I pulled my gear together and saddled the bay.

Captain Simpson looked up at me when I rode up. I did not give him the opportunity to speak. "I'm riding with you, Captain."

A sneer spread across his blubbery face. "Not this time, Mr. Moore. I need no distractions. A white woman has been kidnapped by the Apaches and for all we know, she is being brutalized at this very moment." Holding the pommel with one hand, he steadied the stirrup with the other and hefted his bulk into the saddle. He reined his horse around. It jittered to a stop by Sheriff Black. Simpson glared at me. "Is that clear?"

I studied him. The campfire flickered shadows over his ballooning cheeks. His watery green eyes glowered at me. I deliberately said nothing of her identity. Nothing I could say would change his mind, and I refused to give him the satisfaction of enjoying my anxiety and distress while he lumbered after the Indians in his own sweet time. Without a word, I turned back to my tent. Let him think what he wished.

Later, hoping to get a head start on the patrol, I led the bay into the darkness. A hundred yards outside the bivouac, I mounted. Just before I dug my heels into the pony's flanks, a rider came pounding out of the night, a young Mexican astride a laboring mule. He flashed past a flickering campfire. I glimpsed an arrow protruding from his shoulder before he disappeared into the darkness between fires. When the mule burst into the glow of the next fire, the saddle was empty.

A cluster of men gathered quickly. From where I stood in the rear, I listened in growing apprehension as the youth gasped out the horrors of an Apache massacre at San Pedro, a small village of poor Mexicans twenty miles due south of our encampment. Before he could say more, he passed out.

A cold hand clutched my heart, and a sickening lump formed in my stomach. Was Keen Sighted one of the marauders? I prayed to the sun and moon that he was not.

I believed that once I explained my plan to him, he would cooperate. Then we could manage to settle whatever debt the government felt he owed. But further predations only added to the debt. And at some point, the debt could only be repaid by a life, his life. I had to find him. I glanced to the east. But what about Susan? If we went to San Pedro, she would be taken even farther away from us.

Simpson looked around. His eyes stopped on me. "You can join us this time, Mr. Moore." He snapped an order. "Sergeant, make preparations to move out in fifteen minutes. The entire company. I am declaring an emergency. Lieutenant, call the scouts to my tent." He looked back at me. "You too, Mr. Moore. These murderers, they're your people."

For a moment, I pondered his orders. I put myself in Keen Sighted's shoes. I grunted to myself. Captain R. Albert Simpson had no way of knowing, but a twenty-mule team fresh out of the barn couldn't have kept me from going to San Pedro. Simpson just saved me the trouble of demanding I be allowed to go.

If Standing Bear and Keen Sighted's band had taken Susan, then they would have also taken her with them to San Pedro, for the time between the two raids was not sufficient to permit them to retire to the Santa Catalinas, drop her off at their rancheria, and then swing back west of Tucson.

Simpson had yet to figure out that simple, logistic impossibility. And he would not learn of it from me.

We moved out within the hour. I rode at the rear of the column, preferring the dust in my teeth and the smell in my nostrils to Simpson's endless jabberings. I didn't lie to myself, however. Simpson was just as glad to be rid of me.

If Susan was with Keen Sighted, she was safe. He would die defending her. I believed that simple fact without question. But the distinct possibility was always present that her small group had been hit by an unknown war party passing through Apache country. I chomped at the delay, but for the moment, my mind was made up. San Pedro was where I must first go.

The column moved at a steady pace, four to five miles an hour. Despite my concern that this last raid had pushed the Apache problem beyond a summary solution by local agents, I dozed in the saddle. Sleep had become a rare commodity for me within the last few days.

What little sleep I snatched didn't help much. I don't care what some jaspers say, but about the only thing you gain from sleeping in the saddle is sore kidneys and a crick in the neck.

San Pedro appeared on the horizon an hour after sunrise. Weeping and wailing voices drifted across the desert on the still air. I steeled myself for the scene that lay ahead. Digging my heels into the bay, I rode to the head of the column and pulled in beside Rooney. "You seen anything so far?" I asked, nodding to the trail ahead of us.

"Nothing Apache." He gestured to the east. "They probably rode in from that direction. That's where I figured on cutting sign."

I felt better. Rooney knew what he was doing, although he had much to learn of the Apache. With a nod, I wheeled about and returned to the rear of the column, ignoring the malevolent glare on Simpson's face as I rode past.

The troop had traveled in a somber silence, but as we entered the small village and witnessed graphic evidence of the massacre, the silence was shattered by troopers groaning and throwing up.

Wailing women shrouded in black shawls and children in tattered clothing knelt by the still bodies of husbands and fathers. Stunned parents sat with their dead children in their laps. The savagery had been thorough. From where I sat on the bay, it appeared the Apaches had methodically ransacked each *jacale* and deliberately murdered its inhabitants, leaving bodies strewn behind like leaves fallen from a dying mesquite.

Eighteen to twenty of the wood and mud shacks around an adobe chapel made up the village. I deliberately looked away from the carnage, instead searching for sign of the raiders.

The troop began dispersing, assisting the villagers. Two patrols rode out of the village, one south, the other west. I headed east, careful to stay within sight of the village. The Apache were clever and sneaky. More than once, they had lain in wait for pursuers, knowing that the first few minutes away from the village, the pursuers were least watchful and most vulnerable.

Carefully I covered the two eastern quadrants. Although my tracking skills were rusty, I could still spot the sign of a war party. And I hoped I would not find any sign in that direction. But spot it I did, northeast of San Pedro. I grimaced. More and more, it appeared that this band was Standing Bear's.

The raiders left by the same route as they had come in. The sign was mixed, making it difficult to determine numbers, but I discovered a shallow arroyo off the trail a mile outside of the village where the war party had hidden prior to their attack.

I dismounted and studied the sign in the arroyo. Sixteen to eighteen ponies, I guessed. Looking up from where I was crouched by a set of hoofprints, I studied the low-lying silhouette of the Santa Catalinas to the northeast across the basin. The tracks pointed directly for the mountains. I shook my head. That's where Keen Sighted and Standing Bear had been holed up.

Disappointed, I mounted and headed back to the village, trying to convince myself that the raiders could have been another band of Indians. Who knows? I told myself. A few miles out, the trail could swing back north or east. It could still be Paiute or Comanche.

But I couldn't convince myself.

I found Simpson and his entourage in the chapel. Rooney Catlett was with them. A black-frocked priest lay on a grass pallet, his once swarthy face sallow with impending death. His breathing came in ragged gasps.

Lieutenant Irons was kneeling by the priest, holding

a cup of water to the old man's quivering lips. The old priest shook his head, and Irons withdrew the water.

"Who did it, Padre?" Simpson asked, lowering his voice in an effort to keep the squeak out of it.

The old priest's throat worked. He tried to speak, but only garbled words stumbled from his lips.

I found myself hoping he would say nothing. But then, I remembered the words Chato had once spoken to both Keen Sighted and me. "The feathers of the straight arrow are truth and honesty."

There have been times when I forgot Chato's words, but always they came back as they did now, and a sense of shame burned my cheeks. I wanted the padre to speak, to speak the truth.

Irons lay his hand on the padre's shoulder. "Who did this, Padre? Apache?"

The old man nodded. His dark, unseeing eyes suddenly glittered with a sparkling intensity, as if he had witnessed a vision. "A-Apache. The one . . ." A spasm of coughing wracked his body. A trickle of blood dribbled out the side of his lips and down his neck. "The one they call . . . Keen Sighted."

Chapter Twelve

I closed my eyes and leaned back against the cool adobe. My hopes and prayers were shattered. When I opened my eyes, Captain Simpson was staring at me with a satisfied smirk on his round, sweaty face.

Frustration boiled up inside. I wanted to smash the gloating sneer from his face. "Captain," I said in a low, strained voice as I struggled to contain my anger. "The smartest thing in the world you can do right now is keep your mouth shut."

The sneer faded quickly. I spun on my heel and left the chapel. Outside, I woodenly mounted the bay and rode north to the outskirts of the small village where I awaited the troop.

The padre's dying words just about sealed my own dreams in a coffin of their own. I still grasped at a flicker of hope that I could salvage Keen Sighted, but one more incident would be the shovel that began burying that coffin.

While I awaited the troop, I considered taking up pursuit on my own, but I had no supplies. The smartest move on my part was to return to camp, stock up, and move out that night. What the captain didn't know wouldn't hurt him, and the mood I was in, I didn't care if it did or not.

We reached camp just before sundown. As I rode up, a medical orderly hurried up to me. ''There's an Injun over here, Mr. Moore. He wants to talk to you. He's shot up right bad. I don't figure he's got too long to live.''

Dismounting quickly, I hurried to the medical tent. There, lying in the dirt outside the tent, sprawled the Indian on his back. Apache, I saw immediately.

Bright red blood seeped from wounds in his abdomen and chest. I shot a hard look at the orderly. ''What's he doing out here? Why isn't he in bed?''

The orderly looked at me like I was loco. ''But . . . but, he's an Injun.''

I shoved the orderly aside and scooped up the Apache and carried into the tent where I lay him on a cot. ''He's a man,'' I said, my words a hiss. ''Get me some water.''

''Yes, sir,'' said the young orderly, hopping to obey my command.

Kneeling by the cot, I studied the Apache's face. He looked familiar. The orderly brought the water, and I held the wounded man's head and touched the cup to his parched lips. He sipped the cool water, and a siege of coughing wracked his body.

I laid him back, and he opened his eyes. A weak smile parted his lips. His eyes knew me. "*Ah-han-day.* It is good you are home."

Then I recognized him. "Black Cloud?" I glanced at his wounds. "Who did this?"

Footsteps sounded behind me, but I ignored them. The answer he gave was not what I expected. "Your brother, Keen Sighted."

He tried to focus his eyes on me. His hand sought mine. "He is loco. He kills without thought. He believes all Standing Bear tells him. I try to stop him, make him listen. You . . ."

A rattling cough cut off his words. I lay my hand on his shoulder. "Easy, Black Cloud. The doctor will make you better. Then we can talk."

"No. You must listen. Keen Sighted hears only the winds of hate. You must make him hear you. You . . ." His fingers dug into my hand. "You . . . must . . ." He coughed. His eyes glazed. His fingers dug deeper into my flesh, and then suddenly went limp.

As I sat looking down at Black Cloud, the blood stopped oozing from his wounds. I laid a hand on his chest. His heart beat no longer.

A voice from behind my shoulder startled me. "I hope you're convinced now, Mr. Moore. I tried to tell you, but you were too stubborn to listen."

There was no mistaking the high-pitched voice. Struggling to contain the anger surging through my veins, I rose slowly and turned to face Captain Simpson and Lieutenant Irons. I disliked facing them as much as I did the dark truth Black Cloud had spoken, but both the truth and the officers were before me.

I had to deal with them and with the truth. I had no choice. Keen Sighted was guilty. "I still have a job to do, Captain. And I'm going to do it."

"Oh?" Simpson arched an eyebrow. "What do you propose, Mr. Moore? Are you convinced now that what I have been telling you is the truth? That brother of yours is a murderer who should be shot down like a dog."

Lieutenant Irons muttered. "Please, Captain."

I ignored Irons's words as I glared at Captain Simpson. "I set out to bring Keen Sighted in. I still plan on doing that very thing, but right now, I'm more concerned about the white woman who was kidnapped. Once she's safe, then I'll take care of the Apache."

Simpson frowned. "You seem unusually interested in this woman, Mr. Moore."

"I am. Her name is Susan Leslie. I've known her for twenty years." I started to tell him more, that she was on the wagon with me when the Apaches took us, and that Susan was the only white family I'd ever had, but I decided not to speak of her to him. He didn't deserve to know.

Lieutenant Irons swallowed and glanced uncomfortably at Simpson, whose fat cheeks beamed with satisfaction. "Strange," he mused, finding humor in my words. "The report gave no name."

"That's not surprising."

"But, you . . . you know. How is that, Mr. Moore?" He fancied himself toying with me, but all he was really doing was grating upon my growing irritation.

"I just know, Captain. Just leave it at that."

"From one of his Apache friends, no doubt," he

said to Irons with a sneer. He turned back to me. "So, she was raised by the Apache also."

"That's right." I stepped around him. "Now, if that's it, I've got work to do."

He grabbed my arm and spun me around. Irons looked at him in surprise. Simpson yelled. "No, that is not it. You are going nowhere. I gave you an order. You will answer me, or you will remain in camp until I say so. I asked you how you know her name, and as far as I'm concerned, that squaw girl can stay out there with those other savages for the rest of her—"

Captain R. Albert Simpson did not finish his sentence.

The remaining layer of white civilization slid off my shoulders, and I busted him right in the teeth, breaking two off at the gums and splitting his fat lips. He fell back over the dead body of Black Cloud and tumbled to the ground between the cot and the side of the tent.

Glaring at Irons, who dropped his gaze and stared at the ground, I turned and headed back to my tent. I was fed up with this entire mess. Word spread fast of what I had done, but I ignored it all as I threw my gear together in preparation to pulling out. While tying my gear behind the cantle, Lieutenant Irons approached with six armed troopers.

Now what? I thought to myself, continuing lashing down my gear. But I knew.

"Mr. Moore?"

"What is it now, Lieutenant?"

He hesitated. "Mr. Moore?"

I looked around. "What?"

A look of true regret twisted his angular face. "Mr.

Moore, I'm sorry, but the captain has ordered you to be placed under arrest for assaulting him.''

I stared at him coolly. Slowly I turned to face him, my arms at my side. ''Is that right?''

He nodded. ''That's what he said, Mr. Moore. I . . .'' He shrugged. ''The captain has ordered me to take you to the jail in Tucson.''

For some reason I didn't have time to discern, Lieutenant Irons's heart wasn't in the arrest. I didn't know what had happened to change his mind, but I didn't care. All I knew was that they would not take my guns. My mind was made up. ''Do what you have to do, Lieutenant, but I'm not handing my guns over to you. You've got to take them, and I promise you, someone is going to die.''

The six troopers remained behind the lieutenant, fear in their eyes. Behind them, Rooney Catlett and Big Bow watched and listened silently.

I caught Rooney's eye. He grinned. He didn't know what I planned to do, but he knew I needed a diversion. And he gave me one. He turned to Big Bow and said in a loud voice, ''Look at that owl. I bet I can hit it.'' He raised his Winchester and tore off half a dozen shots in rapid succession.

The lieutenant and his troopers spun. I swung into the saddle and gave a Confederate war cry and drove the bay straight at the lieutenant and his men. They spun back, and barely leaped out of the way as I tore past, lying low over the neck of my horse.

Several shots rang out, but none came close, making me wonder just how anxious Irons and his men had been about taking me to Tucson. But now, at least one thing was certain. I was a man wanted by the military.

Assaulting an officer. Escaping from custody. More than enough for Simpson to file charges. He'd probably even figure out a way to add treason to the charges.

But none of that mattered now. What did matter was finding Susan and Keen Sighted. My first stop would be the fork in the trail to Fort Bowie. That was where Susan had been kidnapped. Perhaps I could find some answers there. If not, then I would have to go into the Santa Catalinas for Keen Sighted. If the Apaches had taken her, she would be safe. If not, then I would try to enlist my brother's help in finding her.

Once Susan was safe, I would then decide what to do about Keen Sighted. I muttered a dark oath at my own mixed feelings; profound beliefs I had once believed to be founded in bedrock were now balanced on the fulcrum of uncertainty.

Simpson's arrogance, his pathetic ignorance of the West, made me want to ride away and forget all about the white man. For the first time since I returned from Washington, I seriously considered ignoring my orders. Who would care?

The vast, blind bureaucracy would mill about for a while, then it would forget all about us. Keen Sighted and I would simply be another dot at the end of one of the many sentences in the history of the West. After a couple years, no one would miss us, no one would know, no one would care.

But I would care. John Salmon Cook would care. Keen Sighted's raids had murdered the innocent also. Nowhere in the great scheme of life with the buffalo and the forest could I find justification for such random killing. No one can blame a man for slaying an enemy who was trying to kill him, but women and children and old men . . . I shoved the bloody images of San Pedro from my mind.

I rode hard, swinging wide into the foothills of the Santa Catalinas until I had passed Tucson. False dawn lit the sky. I cut back southeast, paralleling the Catalinas, hoping to cut the trail near the Fort Bowie fork. Glancing over my right shoulder toward the adobe village of Tucson, I wondered just how far I was ahead of my pursuit.

A few minutes after dawn, I reached the fork in the trail and studied the sign. As rusty as my tracking skills were, I saw quickly that I would find nothing here other than the bloodstains on the ground. The trail was impossible to separate because the white man's sign erased what few tracks the marauding party left. Moving out a hundred yards or so, I cast in a circle around the site.

In the northeast quadrant of the circle, I found Indian sign, unshod ponies mixed with shod. Between eight and ten ponies, all with riders. The desert wind blowing from the southwest had rounded the sharp edges of the tracks. A couple days old, I guessed. It was hard to tell. To be sure this was the party, I backtracked the trail to the fork in the Fort Bowie road. Leaning forward over the bay's neck, I smoothed his mane. "Looks like we found it, old son. Now we got to figure out what do with it."

The trail led at an unhurried pace into the Santa Catalinas. It was an odd trail, not like any with which I was familiar. Apaches usually tagged after each other, single file, but these riders rode four or five abreast, then single file, then others wandered away from the trail only to return a mile farther on. Slowly the trail swung southeast, away from the Santa Catalinas.

The morning sunlight glistened off an object in the trail ahead. I reined up. I was on the edge of the saw-grass and cholla desert, several hundred yards from any possible ambush, but even in such an unlikely spot, the Apache could hide until his victim stepped within an arm's length.

I studied the lay of land around the shiny object; then, satisfied, I clicked my tongue and rode forward. Leaning from my saddle, I scooped up a tiny silver bell. Woven horsehair ran through the small loop on top. A sardonic grin curled my lips. I tinkled the bell. "So much for the Apache war party," I said to the bay. The bell identified the tribe, Comanche.

My spirits rose momentarily, for the bell indicated that Keen Sighted was not one of this party, but they sank quickly when I realized that the only reason Comanche did not kill white women was because they sold them to the Comancheros, who carried the women into Mexico where they were forever lost.

Dropping from the saddle, I studied the ground. The grass was bent. I straightened a shoot of grass, and the tip broke off at the seam. Studying the broken end, I saw that it was dry, which fit in with my guess of two days.

I mounted and studied the trail as it meandered southeast.

Over my left shoulder sprawled the Santa Catalinas, probably as likely a spot to contact Keen Sighted as I could hope to find. I weighed my options. I wasn't a young *ish-kay-nay* out to count coup. There was no way I could surprise ten Comanches. With a shrug, I reined the roan back to the east. I needed help, and the nearest help was Keen Sighted and his Apache renegades.

The mountains of Arizona Territory are unlike those of other ranges. While cataclysmic upheavals forced the serrated peaks high into the clouds in the northern territory and beyond, nature played games with those in the south, forming not a solid line of mountains, but instead a series of mountain ranges interrupted by basins ten, twenty, thirty miles in width, and then another range of mountains, and then another basin, continuing this chain of mountain and basin into the Sierra Madres of Mexico.

I made my way cautiously to the nearest peak and built a smoky fire from which a column of white smoke churned into the cloudless sky. Unless I missed my guess, I had about an hour to spare before the first Apache put in an appearance.

After picketing the bay in a middle of a shelf with some rough browse, I put coffee on to boil and tossed two cups on the ground by the fire. Next to the cups, I placed a bag of sugar and a can of milk, two delicacies eagerly sought by many Indians.

From time to time, I fed the fire, maintaining a steady stream of smoke. I shielded my eyes against the sun and studied the desert between me and Tucson, then south and west to the blue shadows of the Sierrita Mountains. Nothing. I nodded with satisfaction. Either Rooney and Big Bow were guiding the pursuit away from me, or Simpson had decided I wasn't worth the trouble. But I found it very difficult to believe the latter.

The fragrant aroma of fresh coffee filled the air. I poured a cup and squatted with my back to a boulder near the picketed bay. A few feet to my left, the edge of the shelf overlooked a sheer hundred-foot drop.

I looked up when a rock clattered down below. I leaned back and tried to relax, at the same time slipping the rawhide loop off the hammer of my .45. Company was coming, and I wanted to be ready to welcome them. With each passing second, my muscles wound tighter, like a watch spring ready to snap.

Then I heard the sharp click on shod hooves against granite. I poured out the remainder of my coffee and tossed the cup on the ground by the fire. Rising, I kicked a few logs from the fire. The blaze had drawn me some Apache. I just hoped they were the right ones.

When I looked around, two Apache stood less than twenty feet from me, battered Springfields resting in the crook of their arms. I nodded to the coffee. "I am A Long Way, brother to Keen Sighted. You are welcome. Here is coffee."

Neither Apache moved. A third emerged from the trail, coming to stand beside the first two. They eyed me suspiciously. For several moments, we stared at each other.

My bay nickered. I looked around to see an Apache pulling himself over the rim of the shelf. When I looked back, the other three had the muzzles of their rifles trained on me.

"Why do you do this?" I asked. "I come as brother to Keen Sighted. I made you coffee."

The four looked at each other. With a nod, one turned and trotted back down the trail. Moments later, the sound of hoofbeats echoed up the mountainside. One of the Apache motioned for me to sit.

While we waited, they drank the coffee, stirring in a handful of sugar and a surplus of canned milk. An hour later, Keen Sighted rode into camp alone, his face dark and angry.

I rose and faced him. He glared at me from atop his horse, a pinto. His obvious anger did not surprise me.

"How is my brother?" I asked.

He grunted. "You have no brother," he said harshly.

He was referring to the ambush. "Then who was it who shoved you from the path of the soldier's bullet?" I patted the back of my head. "Who was it who took the soldier's bullet intended for you?"

The resolute frown faded from his face. I nodded and showed him the back of my head. "Look." I pointed to the faint scar. "I got that when I shoved your worthless hide out of the way."

Keen Sighted glared at the tone in my voice, but when he saw the grin on my face, he shrugged. "You are white. I think much of you and wonder if your heart has become white."

I gestured to the coffee. "Sit. Let us speak as brothers."

He waved the others away. We sat and drank the remaining coffee.

Clearing my throat, I said, "It is hard for me also, for my heart is both Apache and white. But you are my brother, and though we must speak with each other to know how we feel, that must wait. I have come to you for help. The Comanche have stolen Susan, *Sons-*

ee-ah-ray, our Morning Star. They carry her to the south. To Comancheros, I think.''

Keen Sighted's thick, dark eyebrows knitted, and his broad forehead wrinkled with deep creases. ''When?''

I held up two fingers. ''Two days now.'' I pointed to the south. ''I know the trail. They are ten. That is why I came to you.''

Without hesitation, Keen Sighted rose to his feet and called his men. The three Apache materialized out of the surrounding landscape. He looked at me. ''There are five of us now. Now, the Comanche must fear.''

I nodded.

Keen Sighted extended his first two fingers and touched his lip. He hesitated. I caught my breath, my eyes fixed on his gestures. Was this the sign I had awaited from him? He drew his hand back and extended the forefinger to the sky.

The Indian sign for *brother*. I nodded solemnly, and made the sign myself.

We looked deep into each other's eyes. The feelings we shared as boys still lived.

Chapter Thirteen

We cut the Comanches' sign before dusk. Keen Sighted studied the trail from his saddle, his sharp eyes missing nothing. As a youth, his eyes were like telescopes, and they had lost nothing with age.

"Eleven," he said, giving me a wry grin. "The white man has made you careless, my brother."

"I was close," I protested, returning his grin. "I counted ten."

"Seven unshod. Four Mexican."

"How far?" I asked, looking down the trail.

"Two days." The other Apache grunted and nodded.

One spoke up. "They do not hurry."

Another said. "They fear nothing. They must be brave warriors."

Keen Sighted grinned, his eyes half-closed in amusement. "The Comanche dogs do not know what

131

brave warriors are until they meet the Apache. When we finish, they will scurry from the desert like whipped dogs, dragging their tails between their legs.''

That night and until noon the next day was a familiar but torturous replay of Apache tenacity and conditioning. More than once as youths, we had been forced to undertake a twenty-mile run with a mouthful of water. At the end of the run, before the great warriors of our tribe, we spit out the water, without a drop missing. Those of us who achieved that level of willpower and self-discipline were hailed as future warriors, but those who did not were shamed, and ignored by parents, by family, by the tribe.

By now, we had traveled eighteen straight hours throughout the night and morning, galloping two hours on horseback, running one afoot, leading our ponies. I fell behind each time we dismounted and ran, but I managed to catch Keen Sighted during the next part of the cycle. The longer we rode, the more confident I became. With Keen Sighted at my side, there was nothing we could not accomplish.

At noon, we hid our ponies in a shallow arroyo and snaked to the crest of a gentle rise on our bellies. To the southeast rode the Comanche in a gentle canter, lazily taking their time crossing hostile territory. One thing I had to say for them, they had all the faith in the world in their own prowess.

Keen Sighted grunted and looked at me, his usually impassive face wreathed with concern. ''She is not there. Three horses are missing.''

I grimaced. ''During the night,'' I whispered. ''We missed the trail during the night.''

He started to rise. ''We go back.''

''No.'' I laid my hand on his arm, staying him. I nodded to the Comanche on the prairie before us. ''They will tell us the destination of the missing Comanche.''

Keen Sighted saw the wisdom of my words. He looked at his men, and as one, we rose and dashed to our ponies. With a savage yell, Keen Sighted raced over the crest of the rise with the rest of us right behind him.

The Comanche spotted us. For a moment, they milled about uncertainly, but when they saw they outnumbered us eight to five, they echoed our own wild screams and drove their war horses to meet us.

I unsheathed my Winchester, thankful for its sixteen-round magazine. The balanced weapon was shiny and worn from use, and it had done me well for the five years I had owned it.

Sage blurred, and the prairie rushed past under the pounding hooves of our ponies. Slowly the oncoming Comanche grew larger. When their yells reached our ears over the throbbing beat of our horses, I rose in my stirrups and drew down on the Comanche at the rear of their charge. Kill the ones at the rear. Those in front have no idea what is happening, just like turkeys or ducks. Take the last one, and work forward.

I lined my sights on him. We both were moving in rhythm with our galloping horses, so I had to anticipate where he would be. A puff of smoke billowed from one of the Comanche rifles. I squeezed off my shot. The Comanche ducked and glanced over his shoulder. I missed, but the slug must have zipped close.

He swerved to his left, and I fired again. This time,

luck dealt me a good hand, for my slug knocked him off his pony, which continued galloping across the prairie.

More shots rang out as the Comanche, excellent horsemen they were, sat glued to their war horses, firing at us. Slugs hummed past.

The two charging war parties met, sluiced through each other like water through a net, and spun around for another charge. I snapped off a shot at a Comanche whose pony was jittering around on him. The two-hundred-grain slug knocked him backward off his horse.

A blistering fire burned my thigh, and my bay whinnied and reared. I fought for control, and then drove him into the thick of the melee of horses and riders. Dust rose and enveloped us. We were too close now for rifles. I used the barrel of the Winchester for a club until it was knocked from my hand.

Keen Sighted fought like a demon, screaming and swinging his war club. A heavy weight struck me from behind, and then rolled away. I jerked around to see a Comanche, tomahawk in hand, sag to the ground, a knife protruding from his back. I glanced around to see one of the Apache grinning at me.

In the next instant, a horseman slashed between us, driving a lance through the chest of the Apache who had saved my life. A blinding rage burst in my brain. Viciously, I dug my heels into the bay's flanks, driving him after the Comanche, an insatiable lust for revenge blinding me. I tore my knife from its sheath, and with a cry of vengeance, leaped onto the Comanche's horse, landing on the pony's haunches.

I wrapped one arm around the Comanche's neck

and drove my double-edged knife into his chest with my other. His rigid body went limp, and I pushed him off the galloping pony.

Then, I yanked on the reins, jerking the small pony around so I could rejoin the battle. Blood pounded in my ears. I screamed. A wild excitement coursed through my muscles as I drove the pony into the thick of the fight, bowling over a Comanche pony and sending its rider sprawling to the ground. The brave bounced to his feet, but I had spun my pony and in the moment the Comanche turned to face me, I ran over him.

Suddenly, the fight was over.

Chest heaving, I sat slumped on the Comanche pony, taking in the dead sprawled over the now silent prairie. I was suddenly aware of the sun beating down, baking my shoulders.

I looked at the knife still grasped in my hand. Blood covered the glistening blade. It was hard to believe that hand had once extended from the sleeve of a freshly starched uniform and had held the delicate hands of gracious women wearing sequined and jeweled gowns at holiday balls.

I wiped the blade on my denim trousers, adding bloodstains to the ground-in dirt. Washington, D.C., seemed worlds away. Had I ever really lived in a place called Washington, D.C.? Or had it all been a dream as I slept in the darkness of a cave?

One of our party was dead. Of the survivors, I suffered the only injury, a graze across the top of my thigh. While I tended it, Keen Sighted elicited the information we sought from one of the mortally wounded Comanche by threatening mutilation upon his death. The dying brave, fearing, as did all Indians, that disfiguration would prevent recognition in the Afterworld, gave Keen Sighted the information he sought.

Two Comanche were taking Susan to sell to a band of Comancheros who had recently left Arizpe bound for the Baboquivaris. Keen Sighted nodded and rose to his feet.

With a groan, the Comanche lay back and died.

An Apache advanced, his knife drawn, intent on mutilation, but Keen Sighted stopped him. "He can hurt us no longer. Let him enjoy wherever it is Comanches go."

He glanced at me, and I nodded at his decision.

"You are well?" He nodded to my wound.

"The mosquito stings more than this," I replied.

"Good." He knelt by the dead Apache and signaled to one of the Apache who rounded up a pony. Keen Sighted gently draped the single dead Apache over the pony. Somewhere, we would find a proper place to bury him. Keen Sighted spoke to an Apache named Little Dog who swung astride his pony and, with another Apache, headed back to the Santa Catalinas.

When Keen Sighted saw the question in my eyes, he explained. "Little Dog brings help."

"But why?" I argued. "We were four. The Comanche are two."

"Who can say where they meet the Comancheros, my brother." A lazy grin played over his dark face. He tapped his forehead. "Be wise like the owl. Do not worry. We waste no time. Little Dog and the others will catch us."

We rode out minutes later, angling to the southwest

to cut the Comanche sign. Over a hundred miles to the south lay the sleepy village of Arizpe. Somewhere on that hot and dusty trail between that village and the Baboquivari Mountains rode Susan. And I was determined to find her.

For the present, she was safe. The Comanche would take good care of her, for she was worth at least three Winchesters and two hundred rounds. But, if they should discover they were being followed, they would forget the Winchesters and kill her.

By dusk, we had not found their trail. The possibility, however slim, that they altered their plans, or that the dying Comanche had lied, nagged at us. We must wait until morning. We could take no chances on missing the trail in the dark.

Despite our impatience, we camped, first burying our dead friend. We then built a small fire and rested, chewing jerky and sipping warm water. We had nestled down in a water-cut hollow beneath a slight overhang in the bend of an arroyo.

For the first time in eleven years, Keen Sighted and I were alone, brother to brother. It seemed strange. I told him so.

He grinned, his teeth brilliantly white against his dark skin. "I, too, feel as you. But it is natural. We have been from each other's life for these last many years."

We talked of our family, reminisced of our youth, and wondered of our future. I told him of my dreams for a ranch for the three of us.

Excitement glittered in his eyes when I described the towering mountains, their slopes bulging with game, their sweet, cold streams filled with fat fish, and their valleys thick with lush grass.

He glanced at the sand at our feet and frowned up at me. "It is hard to believe such a place exists. That is how the life after is to be, all of us with our fathers and their fathers, living a life without the white man."

"It does exist," I said. "I bought it. For us. For you, and Susan, and me."

A grin spread over his rugged face. "You would do well to take her as your woman and raise fine children on the ranch."

I leaned forward and laid my hand on his shoulder. "It's for the three of us. And we can go there whenever we want. As soon as we free Susan, we can go."

He smiled and leaned back, his eyes amused. "And what about the reason you are here?"

I sensed I had reached a turning point, a time when I made a decision that would change the course of my life. The moment was frightening, but strangely exciting. "You. You are that reason."

"Yes. You told me once that questions needed answers, and once the answers were given, all would be over."

I grunted. "I was wrong. I don't believe answers will help. I think Washington wants the answers, but the men they send for the answers, the bluecoats, they speak words that are like a crooked arrow."

Keen Sighted said nothing. He just looked at me with dark, sad eyes. I continued. "I came here from Washington, hoping you would go with me to answer these questions, but now, I cannot ask."

"Because you know I have killed? And because you

know also that those who spoke of me to you did not lie?''

I started to agree, but the words stuck in my throat. I shrugged.

He studied me, then lay back on the sand. He spoke with gentle tolerance as if he were pacifying an excited child. ''I am not unhappy. I am not sad. I have done that which I must. I have remained true to my beliefs. You can do no less. Now, sleep. We have much to undertake before we can do any of these grand things of which you speak.''

Sleep was long in coming. Confused thoughts tumbled through my head. I was in the middle of a tug-of-war between two cultures, each believing its way best. But neither suited everyone, only those who adhered to those particular beliefs.

So how did I come to believe I could find an answer that would satisfy both sides?

I refused to admit there was no solution. There had to be one somewhere, one both sides would accept. I fell asleep struggling for the answer.

The vibration of hoofbeats awakened me. The sky was still dark. Keen Sighted stood on the rim of the arroyo, peering to the north. ''Is it them?'' I whispered.

''Yes,'' he replied, leaping easily from the rim to the sandy bed of the arroyo. ''We go now.''

Mounted, we awaited our reinforcements in the crisp air of predawn. Keen Sighted spoke without looking at me. ''One day, my brother, we will follow your dream.'' He turned to me and laid his hand on my shoulder. ''You and me, we are Apache. Do not forget the words of our father. An Apache must face that which the spirits have ordered for him. There is much you must do. But there is also much I must do. How can we not?'' A great sadness filled his eyes. He shrugged. ''What else is there?''

With a sinking heart, I understood his words. He was right. Deep inside me where the private voice lives, I knew he was right. But I couldn't admit it. It hurt too much.

A shout broke into my thoughts. Keen Sighted frowned as a dozen Apache led by Little Dog rode up. Among them was Strong Swimmer, the leader of the small band of Apaches I met earlier and a young boy, an *ish-kay-nay*. Keen Sighted called the *ish-kay-nay* to us. ''Why are you here? There are no horses to herd.''

The young boy gulped, but held his eyes on those of Keen Sighted. ''I am Apache. I can fight as well as the others.''

Keen Sighted glared at him, but in the cool light of the fading stars, I could see pride scribed across my brother's face. He said to me. ''This whelp is Young Eagle, son of Colored Beads, brother to *Sons-ee-ah-ray*. He is like a flea, always making me itch. He goes where he is not wanted.''

Surprised, I looked at the grinning young man, unable to believe he was only a toddler when I left. Now, he was a fine-looking young boy with clean features and a bright smile. I spoke with disbelief. ''He was no more than a child when I left.''

''That was many years ago, A Long Way,'' Young Eagle replied, his voice breaking slightly. ''Much happens in that time.''

I laughed and remembered Susan. I grinned as I

thought just how excited she would be to know her younger brother still lived.

Keen Sighted shook his head. "Young Eagle is like a worrisome puppy. Always he wants to tag after me."

"To keep the old man from hurting himself," Young Eagle replied, not to be outdone in the friendly banter.

"Just remember," Keen Sighted warned. "The Comanche believes his life is well lived if he dies with an Apache scalp in his belt." I saw the look of concern on his face.

Young Eagle nodded eagerly. "It is the Comanche who must worry." He struck his chest lightly with his fist. "I, Young Eagle, will strike fear to his heart."

Keen Sighted shook his head and looked at me. "I sometimes think it would have been better if the eagle had carried him off."

I grinned. "Perhaps he did and dropped the *ish-kay-nay* on his head."

Keen Sighted laughed.

We spoke with Little Dog. Keen Sighted wanted more braves, but Little Dog informed us that Standing Bear had refused to come. Instead, he had led the other braves to Mexico.

Keen Sighted glanced at me, then quickly looked away, but not before I saw the suspicion written across his face. I nodded to myself. Standing Bear had bolted, leaving Keen Sighted behind to face the bluecoats.

Two hours later, we cut the Comanche trail, three sets of tracks. They were less than six hours ahead.

Chapter Fourteen

We rode hard, steadily gaining on the Comanche. Far to the south, the Sierra Madres peeked over the horizon, growing ever larger as we continued pursuit. The three sets of tracks maintained their original direction. They still traveled slowly and without alarm.

Keen Sighted reined up. We milled about him as he studied the ground before us. "They do not hurry." He frowned. "In a strange land, they act as if it belongs to them." His frown deepened. He looked at me. "I think they meet the Comancheros soon."

"But the mountains are still a day's ride," I replied, nodding to the dark line of mountains silhouetted against a sky blue as the egg of the robin.

"Today. Perhaps even as we speak, they meet."

Two or three voices behind us urged a frontal attack. "No," I said to Keen Sighted. "We don't know what they will do to Susan."

142

He agreed. "We will follow the trail, but we must be cautious as the rabbit fleeing the hawk."

The desert surrounding us was flat as any tableland, but mesquite and spidery ocotillo and majestic saguaro rose thickly from the scrub covering the desert floor, providing deep pockets of undergrowth and protection. This was no desert where the eye sees for miles, but one where the enemy may be hiding behind the next patch of thick mesquite or tightly woven copse of cholla and barrel cactus.

We spread out, moving forward four and five abreast, skirting the patches of cactus and mesquite. The hair on the back of my neck prickled. I rubbed it, expecting to find my fingers wet with sweat, but they were dry. I scanned the desert ahead of us, sensing danger, but seeing only patches of cactus and mesquite spreading across the desert to the foothills of the Sierra Madres.

Several hundred yards ahead, a thick cluster of saguaro and mesquite the size of a two-story house rose from the desert. Keen Sighted glanced at me. I nodded. A perfect spot for an ambush, the patch was large enough to shield twenty warriors from view. Smaller patches of prickly pear and hedgehog cactus surrounded the saguaro and mesquite as far as the eye could see.

We broke into two parties, each moving to skirt the large patch of saguaro and trap anyone who might be there between us. I pulled my .45 and inserted a cartridge in the empty chamber. I spun the cylinder and cocked the hammer.

Slowly we eased forward. A hundred yards ahead, the thicket sat darkly, silently. The sun struck the white sand and bounced back in my eyes with such intensity that I had to squint against the glare. Behind me, I heard the sounds of cartridges being chambered, of bows being strung and arrows nocked.

I kept the reins tight, the horse gathered, ready for instant action. Tense as he was, the pony jittered nervously and tugged at the reins. We were within fifty yards of the thicket now, and at any moment, I expected the silence to be ripped apart with gunfire, but still, only the distant chirruping of crickets broke the still air.

A tiny sparrow darted from the underbrush, and on the other side, a skittish rabbit dashed away from us. A wave of relief swept over me, for if anyone had been hiding behind the underbrush, the bird and rabbit would have already spooked. But at the same time, a nagging worry continued to pick at me.

On the far side of the thicket, Keen Sighted paused. He nodded, and slowly we eased forward, muscles tense, guns ready. Within seconds, we would know. I clenched my teeth, ready to move the instant I heard the first shot. But all remained silent.

Ten yards now. Still nothing.

With one last, excruciating grimace, I rounded the thicket. The only tracks blemishing the smooth sand were the pug marks of rabbits and coyotes and the telltale S tracks of the sidewinder.

Keen Sighted grinned at me.

And then the silence exploded.

Something wet struck my shoulder and head. I looked around to see an Apache beside me tumble from his pony. The air was split by whistling slugs, ripped by wild screams, and shattered by ear-rending explosions.

I spun the bay, thinking they would now kill Susan because they discovered us following them. And then I didn't have time for anything but fighting. Rising from behind the small patches of cholla and prickly pear surrounding the saguaro and mesquite patch, a dozen Indians and as many Mexicans poured volley after volley into our confused band. I had no time to look, but from the sounds behind my back and to my right, Keen Sighted had run into the same fate.

Another Apache screamed and threw out his arms as he was flung backward off his pony. We were badly outnumbered and seriously demoralized by the sudden onslaught. I snapped off two or three shots as I tried to rally the party. A slug tore my hat from my head.

The bay reared on his hind legs. I threw a shot at a Mexican bandit whose face tightened in surprise as he spun to the ground from the slug in his shoulder. I waved the muzzle of my Colt at Keen Sighted. "This way," I yelled, digging my heels into the squealing bay and charging the strength of the ambush, a group of five or six Indians standing shoulder to shoulder.

Leaning low into the bay's mane, I fired under his neck. One of the Indians pitched forward. I snapped off another shot, and then I was on top of them. They leaped aside, opening a hole in the near perfect ambush they had laid for us.

Before they could gather themselves, I was a hundred yards away, followed by Keen Sighted and the remainder of his men. We paused long enough to determine our strength. We were eight now. I looked around hastily, my heart in my throat. I relaxed when

I saw Young Eagle was with us. His youthful face was pale, but his dark eyes glittered with excitement. A slug had grazed his shoulder, leaving a faint red burn.

In the next instant, the desert vibrated with hoof-beats. Keen Sighted and I looked into each other's eyes. We didn't like running, but until we were more certain of the strength we were facing, flight made the best sense.

We headed west, hoping we weren't heading into another trap.

The pursuit followed. For an hour, we raced across the desert, past the towering saguaros that silently watched our flight to safety. Soaked with a heavy lather, our ponies began to labor. A quarter of a mile ahead, a small outcropping of granite protruded several feet above the desert floor. Urging our ponies on, we thundered across the prairie to the protection of the rocky bulwarks.

Upon dismounting, I realized we were no longer being pursued. Keen Sighted looked at me. I shrugged. "I did not look back. I do not know when they stopped following us."

"Nor I," he replied.

We rested, letting our ponies blow. After they cooled, we gave them water.

"Paiute," Keen Sighted announced after we finished tending our animals. "They ride as slaves with the Comancheros."

"Slaves?"

"Of their own choice," he explained. "The Paiute thinks like a snail. He clings to that which feeds him."

I nodded, tired of the talk of the Paiutes. "Susan?

What about Susan and the Comanches who stole her? Do you think she is—''

''No.'' He shook his head. ''She lives. Even now, she is with the Comancheros. Did you not see that the Comancheros were among those who fired upon us.''

''I saw Mexicans.''

''That was them. Two Comanche stood at their side.''

''Do you believe they will return to Arizpe now they have been discovered?'' I asked.

Keen Sighted stared across the desert, which, from our perch on the outcropping, appeared to be covered with a carpet of cactus and mesquite punctuated by the solemn saguaro standing like a solitary sentinel. ''I do not think so. The Comanchero will not return with a single woman, even one who is white.'' He looked around at me. ''No, the Comanchero will continue north where they will barter and raid for more slaves. Then they will return to Arizpe.''

Young Eagle had been listening to us. He spoke up. ''Let us follow now, Keen Sighted. We can take her from the Comancheros.''

My brother considered the request, but he finally shook his head. ''No. They know of us, and they know of our escape, so they expect us to follow. . . .'' He paused, grinned broadly, and added, ''But they will not be expecting us to be waiting for them.''

I grinned at his idea, but Young Eagle frowned. ''I do not understand,'' he said.

Keen Sighted arched an eyebrow at Young Eagle, but spoke to me. ''Maybe the eagle did drop him on his head. What do you think, brother?''

I winked at Young Eagle. ''But perhaps his head is

as the granite.'' I hesitated. ''They still go to the Baboquivaris?''

Keen Sighted grunted. ''You might look like the white man, but you remember like the Apache.'' He nodded. ''Yes. That is where we will wait.''

''But the trail. One of us should stay on the trail. I will follow. You go ahead and wait.''

He pondered my words. ''If they know you follow, they could kill her.''

That possibility was something of which I was well aware. ''But what if they decide not to go to the Baboquivari Mountains, but to the Santa Catalinas or elsewhere?''

With reluctance, he consented. ''Take Little Dog with you.''

I looked at the wiry Apache who was checking the loading action of his Winchester. He nodded to me. We mounted and headed north to intersect the trail as the rest of the party turned west. They planned to skirt the Comancheros and ride ahead to the Baboquivaris.

Just before sunset, Little Dog and I struck the trail of the Comancheros, a set of butcher-knife wheel tracks cutting deep into the sand.

We knelt by our ponies and studied the trail. ''Two hours,'' he said.

Leading our ponies, we followed the tracks until we could no longer see. Then we moved half a mile off the trail and made a cold camp. Later the moon rose.

We rose with the false dawn and made our way back to the trail. We froze in our tracks when we reached the trail. There, over our tracks from the night before were four sets of moccasin prints, made during the night.

I looked at Little Dog. His thoughts were as mine. Mounting, we backtracked to the point at which we had discovered the trail the afternoon before. Where our own sign met the trail, a number of moccasined tracks milled about.

Obviously, the Indians had discovered our tracks and knew we were following the Comancheros. I grimaced. Why hadn't we followed the trail from a distance?

Little Dog spoke up. "They do not know it was us," he said, hoping to relieve me of my anxiety.

"Who else could it be?"

He shrugged.

We turned back on the trail.

Now that they knew we were following, they would be waiting for us. Not only did we have to watch for ambush, but now we also had given the Comancheros another reason to kill Susan.

We rode some distance from the trail, from time to time, riding in to check its direction. Always, we rode with discretion.

Late that afternoon, we discovered where the Indians had overtaken the Comancheros. The ground was a confused maze of sign. But it appeared that the entire group had moved out together.

Little Dog hesitated, staring at the ground.

"What do you see?"

He looked up at me, then indicated a set of shod tracks. "A white man has joined them."

"Comanchero?"

"I think not."

The identity of the newcomer puzzled me. I looked around the desert surrounding us. If he wasn't a Comanchero, he must be white. Who was he? A drifter? No. Comancheros would split a drifter open. They knew this one. A white man who was friends with the Comancheros.

Little Dog swung onto his pony. "We go."

Our pursuit discovered, we rode between the wagon tracks now. Around each bend, I expected to find Susan, murdered by the Comancheros in a fit of rage. But around each bend, all we discovered was more trail.

The sun paused on the horizon, ready to topple off and drag the night behind it. In the distance, dark specks appeared against the graying sky. A hard lump leaped into my throat. Buzzards!

I dug my heels into the bay's flanks and squinted my eyes into the blazing wind as I streaked across the desert.

Chapter Fifteen

Little Dog heeled his pony after me, but my eyes remained focused on the buzzards lazily circling far ahead. I leaned low over the bay's neck, trying to distribute my weight to eke out every last surge of speed from the animal. Slowly the dusk grew darker.

Visions of unspeakable mutilations burst in my head. I clenched my teeth. If they killed her, they would never know any peace. I would not permit them any. I drove the game little bay through thick underbrush, slashing both of us with sharp thorns and needlelike spines.

The bay swerved around a small clump of cholla and mesquite. I grimaced. Ahead, a dark form lay in the middle of the trail, a vague shadow in the middle of the encroaching darkness. My heart thudded against my chest. I wanted to scream, but the sound was frozen in my throat.

I leaped from the bay and hit the ground running. "Susan!" I slid to a halt. The steady drone of buzzing flies filled the still air. A wave of relief swept over me, followed by a tide of revulsion. The dark hair and skin spoke clearly that the dead body was not that of Susan, but the body was so badly mutilated that even the man's own mother couldn't have identified him. I forced the rising gorge back down my throat.

I looked up at Little Dog, who looked on with idle detachment. "A warning," he said simply.

"To us?"

He nodded. "The woman is next."

I stared at the mutilated body. "Who was he, do you think?"

My Apache companion shrugged. "To the Comanchero, it is of no difference."

Little Dog's implication slowly sank in. I clenched my fists in anger as my sense of outrage exploded. I muttered a dark oath. An example. That's all the unfortunate man was, an example. My fingers gripped the butt of my .45. That the dead man deserved hanging, I had no doubt, but to be senselessly mutilated just as a warning was reprehensible. Had I one of the Comancheros before me at that moment, I don't believe I could have stopped myself from putting a slug between his eyes.

"You cannot follow. Not if you wish the white woman to live."

His words were true. I would do nothing more to endanger her. "Then we swing wide and move north. At Tucson, we will cut west and join Keen Sighted," I said, gesturing in that direction.

"They will believe we have given up, but if we are

lucky, they will not move in our direction for fear of discovery. Instead, they will continue to the Baboquivaris, where Keen Sighted will be waiting for them.''

Little Dog nodded, his face solemn. ''Do not forget. The Comanchero will do as he promises if he thinks you plan to trap him.''

''Then we must give him no reason to believe so.''

I did not like the idea of riding off and leaving Susan, but there was no choice. Either I did as they said, or they killed her.

We rode another mile and reined up. As Little Dog dismounted, his Winchester discharged, a bellowing roar in the silence of the desert. He grimaced and beat the heel of his hand against the receiver. ''When the Paiute ambushed us,'' he explained, trying to operate the levering action of the rifle. ''A bullet struck the gun.'' A scar ran the length of the side plate and gouged out a chunk of the grip. Finally, after much pushing and yanking, Little Dog had the action functioning, not smoothly, but at least, operating.

We built a small fire and boiled coffee and ate jerky since we knew our presence was known. The next morning, we saddled up and rode north at an easy gait, knowing that we were being watched. From my saddle, I scanned the desert, filled with wavering images of ocotillo, cholla, and mesquite, but not once did I see any indication of Comancheros or their companion Paiutes and Comanche. But they were out there. Of that, I was certain.

The sun blazed down. Perspiration soaked my clothes. I removed my neckerchief and knotted the corners to fashion a cap against the sun.

I thought of Susan. Where was she at that moment?

Safe? Or had the Comancheros jumped at shadows and killed her? I pushed the thoughts from my head. They served no purpose. Not now.

After crossing the border into Arizona Territory, we continued north, waiting until the sprawling little village of Tucson rose over the horizon before cutting northwest to the Baboquivaris. Not wanting to take any chance our trail would be cut by the Comanchero band, I decided Little Dog and I should enter into the mountains from the north.

We rode hard, spelling the ponies every couple hours by dismounting and leading them at a brisk trot. After a few hours, I was exhausted, but Little Dog could have maintained the pace from sunup to sunup.

The sun dropped behind the Baboquivaris as we reached the northern foothills. I looked anxiously to the south, hoping our loop had been wide enough to mislead the Comancheros. There was no sign of the renegades, no dust, nothing to indicate they were within a dozen miles.

Little Dog led the way through the rugged foothills, ever ascending into the heights of the mountain range as the sky grew dark. From overhead, the slender sickle of the waxing moon illuminated the mountains with a pale glow to guide our steps. Soon the desert lay at our feet as we traversed a narrow ledge clinging to the precipitous granite palisades along the eastern slopes.

Far to the south, a faint light flickered on the desert floor. Little Dog grunted and pointed it out. "They camp tonight. Come in after dawn."

Although I was still worried about Susan, I felt better knowing where they were. Fifteen minutes later, we rode off the ledge and up a broad and gentle slope between two sheer walls of granite, which funneled us into Keen Sighted's camp. Two sentries appeared from the darkness around the mouth of a cave. One of them was Black Wolf, the Apache brave I backed down in the desert my first morning out of Tucson. He glared at me. I ignored him as I studied our backtrail and puzzled over this cave as a meeting place. I hoped the cave had a rear exit, for the lay of the land was such that even a small force could contain an army in the cave.

Inside, Keen Sighted squatted by a small fire. He nodded when we entered and dismounted. An Apache brave took our ponies to an antechamber. "They will be tended," Keen Sighted said. "Come. Eat." Broiling venison popped and crackled on spits stuck in the ground around a small fire. Its succulent aroma assailed my nostrils. My stomach growled. All I had eaten in the last two days had been leather-tough jerky.

Keen Sighted remained sitting by the fire. Shadows danced across his face from the flickering flames. He watched us impassively.

After we made ourselves comfortable, he spoke. "They come in the morning." He made a drawing in the sand. "Two trails lead into the mountains. We will be at each." He punched a hole in the sand at the end of each trail.

I glanced up at him, then counted our numbers. That meant each band would have only four men. I hesitated and glanced at Young Eagle. No. One band would have three men and a boy. "We will be few."

A tense silence filled the cave. A chuckle from the

darkness behind us broke the tension. "We are always few, but we fight like many."

In the darkness, white teeth shone in bright, laughing smiles, a rarity among the usually stoic and unemotional Apache.

Keen Sighted silenced the laughter. "But they are many."

I tore off a chunk of venison with my teeth. "Have you seen them?"

He nodded and pointed to one Apache behind me. "Strong Swimmer saw them this morning. There are *nah-tin-yay*."

At his word, twenty, the venison seemed to grow larger and larger as I chewed. "Twenty of them, and we are only eight?"

"Three white eyes. Two are Comanchero. The other is the sheriff of Tucson."

The sheriff! I shot a glance at Little Dog. He nodded. So that was who joined the Comancheros out in the desert. All that I had heard of Sheriff Samuel Black came back to fill my head with anxiety. As far as I was concerned, he was no better than the Comancheros and just as dangerous.

Keen Sighted pulled his knife and sliced a sliver of venison and popped it in his mouth. "We are here," he said, punching a hole in the sand a few inches north of his previous drawing. He gestured to the rear of the cave. "A passage leads to each of the trails. Before dawn, we will take our places." That answered one of my questions.

"Suppose the Comancheros move out during the night? After all, they knew Little Dog and me were on their trail. They're bound to be spooky."

A knowing grin broke the solemnity of his face. "We watch. We will know if the Comanchero decides to move."

I turned up my canteen and washed the venison down with a large swallow of water. I was still worried about Susan, but Keen Sighted seemed to have the situation well in hand, at least, I cautioned myself, as well as anyone could. I scooted back from the fire and stretched out on the sandy floor.

Keen Sighted spoke. "My brother has made enemies of the bluecoats?"

Raising my head, I looked at him. "You have spies everywhere, I think."

He grinned. "It is wise to know of your enemies." He grew serious. "They say you struck a bluecoat officer and deserted."

I grinned ruefully. That sounded just like the way Captain R. Albert Simpson would have worded it. "Perhaps," I replied.

Keen Sighted studied me several seconds. "The captain has ordered his men to shoot you on sight."

"Perhaps," I replied once again.

A trace of a smile played over Keen Sighted's rugged face. "Sleep. Tomorrow, we fight."

With a cursory nod, I lay back. Moments later, I fell asleep.

I awakened to see the soft gray light of dawn seeping through the thick cloak of the night, gradually illumining the mouth of the cave. The fire was reduced to a bed of blinking coals. Sitting up, I tossed a few pieces of tinder on the coals.

After a moment, faint stringers of smoke slithered into the darkness above the coals. The smoke thickened, and a tiny flame burst forth. I fed more tinder, then twigs followed by larger branches. Within a few minutes, a warm blaze filled the cave.

I rummaged through my gear and put a pot of coffee on to boil, making sure I had enough for all even though the black liquid was not an Apache favorite. I only had two tin cups, so it would have to be a share and share alike.

By the time the coffeepot had been drained and the remainder of the venison bolted down, the sun had lumbered over the desert, stretching the shadowy fingers of mesquite and majestic saguaro across the sand like the spindly fingers of ocotillo.

From the rear of the cave came the sound of moccasins crunching in the sand. Hunkered by the fire, the six of us looked around at the same time. Black Wolf, the sentry, halted and nodded to Keen Sighted. "They come."

Keen Sighted rose and shrugged his massive shoulders. "How long?"

The Apache shrugged. "Soon. By the time the sun is two hands over the desert."

His answer translated into one hour. I glanced at Keen Sighted, who replied, "Which trail do they take?"

Black Wolf shook his head. "It is too soon."

With a curt nod, Keen Sighted turned back to the fire. He pointed to Little Dog and Black Wolf. "You go with my brother, A Long Way." He directed his next words to Little Dog. "Take the trail between the round rocks. I will take my place on the other trail."

Little Dog nodded, and without a word, picked up his rifle and led the way into the rear of the cave. I followed close behind. At places in the passage, it narrowed so that we had to slip sideways between granite walls.

Thirty minutes later, we emerged from the cave onto a ledge black with gold-bearing ore. A young Apache with legs like barrels looked around and nodded at Little Dog. Four hundred feet below, a trail wound between two sharp ridges. Each ridge, the slopes littered with boulders from the size of woven baskets to covered wagons, rose three hundred feet into the air. Little Dog pointed with the muzzle of his Winchester. "If they come our way, that is their trail."

I looked out across the desert. A thin boil of dust rolled up on the horizon. "Is that the Comancheros?"

The young Apache grunted. "I think they come by this trail."

"We will soon know," replied Little Dog, slipping behind a granite boulder overlooking the trail that was still covered with shadows remaining from the night. The sun dappled the crests of the ridges with its first light, then painted a bright, gold line that gradually slipped farther and farther down the ridges, burning away the darkness.

Little Dog and the other Apache quickly disappeared among the boulders on the ridge while Black Wolf remained on the ledge. I studied the trail, noting that a gun on either of the ridge slopes would catch the party in a crossfire. I said, "I will take a place down the ridge. Once the Comancheros pass me, I will signal."

Black Wolf shook his head. "If they do not take this trial, we must move quickly to aid Keen Sighted."

"I know. But I will not be so far that I cannot reach him in time."

Reluctantly he agreed. I climbed down from the ledge and made my way along the crest of the ridge to a cluster of boulders a quarter of a mile from the ledge. Peering from among the boulders, I spotted Black Wolf. We had a perfect ambush set up. Now, all we had to do was make sure we didn't hit Susan.

Slowly the billowing dust grew larger, appearing that it would move past us and turn into the mountains where Keen Sighted waited. I cursed my luck as I started to climb from behind the boulders and hurry to join Keen Sighted.

Then I froze. The dust began moving in my direction. I smiled grimly. Right into our hands.

Soon the battered wagon, a converted Army ambulance, followed by a large number of mounted Paiutes, emerged from the boil of dust. Two Mexicans rode on the bouncing seat, shaded by the cowhide canopy covering the wagon. Behind them, leaning against bulging sacks, Susan slumped in the bed of the wagon. The sheriff forked a mousey dun alongside the wagon.

I looked over my shoulder in time to see Keen Sighted duck behind a boulder near Black Wolf on the ledge. A few feet away, Young Eagle slipped behind another.

We were ready, or I reminded myself, as ready as we could be against almost three-to-one odds. But surprise was on our side. If our first volley could take out three or four, then we had a chance. If not . . .

I refused to consider the idea.

Crouching low as the rattling of the butcher-knife wheels and hooves cut through the sand and clattered over occasional shards of granite lying in the trail, I listened carefully, picking up the creak of leather, the jangle of spurs, the murmur of hushed voices, each new sound bringing them closer.

Gradually the party grew nearer. I flexed my fingers around my own Winchester, letting the air dry my sweaty palms. From their sounds, they were less than fifty yards down the trail.

I planned my first two shots. The two Mexicans on the wagon. I would wait until Black Wolf and Keen Sighted fired from the ledge. While the Comancheros' attention was focused forward, I would catch them from the side. The sheriff would probably bolt and try to escape back down the trail. With luck, during the ensuing confusion, I could make my way down to the wagon and rescue Susan.

I leaned back against the boulder and closed my eyes, pushing the present aside for the moment and trying to visualize our ranch in Wyoming. Immediately, I plunged into a depression.

Keen Sighted. What would happen to him after this?

What could I do about him? He was guilty. No question at all. And he should face a trial. That's why I had been sent back here, to discover the truth. And I did discover it. And I wished I hadn't. So now, what did I do?

Even Keen Sighted told me what I should do. But I couldn't make myself believe it. Deep inside, however, I knew he was right. As he said, an Apache must do that which the spirits have ordered for him. How can we do less than what we must? With a sinking feeling, I realized that Keen Sighted must stand trial.

That was the only way Washington would be satisfied. That was the reason John Salmon Cook gave his life.

A voice echoed up the trail, bouncing from one ridge to the other. I glanced at the ledge. Keen Sighted and his men remained hidden. Easing to my belly, I peered through the branches of some scrub sage at the base of the boulder. The trail was still in shadows for the sun had not yet risen high enough to pour its warmth and light into the depths between the ridges. The Paiutes at the head of the column were passing me. The converted Army ambulance bounced along behind.

Slowly I eased the muzzle of the Winchester beneath the bottom limbs of the sage. The wagon drew even with me. Susan sat slumped in the bed, her chin resting on her chest.

Another minute. That was all we needed. Just one more minute, and then we—

The silence exploded with the roar of a gunshot.

For what seemed like hours, the reverberation of the report echoed across the silent desert. Startled birds squawked and shot into the air. A frightened rabbit darted around a prickly pear cactus and shot into its den at the base of a cluster of rocks. At the top of the far ridge, a deer suddenly appeared, its head held high, its body rigid. Then it bolted over the crest and out of sight. I shot a look at the puff of smoke rising on the opposite ridge, unable to believe my eyes and ears.

Though time dragged for what seemed like hours, only a fraction of a second passed before the mountainside erupted with gunfire. I jammed the butt into my shoulder and tried to draw a bead on one of the

Comancheros in the wagon, but they had both leaped to the ground and were scrabbling behind boulders.

I snapped off a shot. One of the Comancheros twisted sideways as my slug caught him in the back below his left shoulder, but he dragged himself behind a boulder.

From the corner of my eye, I saw Sheriff Black's dun go down, throwing the sheriff behind a boulder.

Slugs ricocheted off the boulders above me. One clipped a branch from the sage. Another struck the ground near my face, peppering my cheek with slivers of granite. I rolled behind a boulder and fired from the other side.

The gunfire from the ledge was murderous. I managed to sneak a look. Susan had leaped from the wagon and was huddled on the ground beneath the bed.

Within brief seconds, the Comancheros and Paiutes had located the source of the onslaught and were returning fire. In the midst of the deadly gunfire, Little Dog, on the opposite ridge, leaped from behind his boulder and dashed back to the ledge. I cursed under my breath. He had given the Comancheros an escape route.

Suddenly, with a sharp yell as a signal, the entire party below moved up the side of the far ridge, hiding among the very boulders Little Dog had fled. Two Comancheros grabbed Susan and dragged her after them. I took careful aim and caught one in the shoulder. He screamed and spun to the ground, kicking his feet frantically in an effort to reach the protection of a boulder. The second Comanchero yanked Susan up in front of him. From out of nowhere, Sheriff Black slipped behind the Comanchero. Together, the two men backed slowly up the ridge, holding Susan as a shield.

The firing continued unabated. Slugs hummed and whistled from all directions, like bees buzzing a broken jar of honey. Ricochets whined off the boulders, thudded into the ground. The Apache on the ledge had moved as the Paiutes and Comancheros fanned out on the slopes of both ridges.

Fifty yards below the crest of the far ridge, two Paiutes joined the Comanchero and the sheriff. I scanned the ridge slopes back to my left. A hundred yards down the trail, a cluster of boulders butted against the trail. Quickly I scooted down the backside of the ridge on which I lay. Rising into a crouch, I ran along the slope until I guessed I was even with the boulders.

Remaining low, I eased over the ridge and, using the sparse undergrowth clinging to the cracks in the granite slope, slipped down to the boulders. As I reached them, I saw the two men disappear over the top of the adjacent ridge with Susan. The Paiutes followed.

Ignoring the slugs whizzing past, I scrambled straight up the far ridge, fearful of losing sight of them. At the top, I crouched among a tumble of rocks. I glanced over my shoulder toward Tucson. A cloud of dust lay on the horizon, but the bright sun was too piercing for me to discern the source of the cloud.

I forgot about the dust. I peered down the slope. Black and the Comanchero were running along a twisting path, dragging Susan after them. The Paiutes followed, directing their fire on Keen Sighted's posi-

tion. An Apache rose from behind a clump of cedar
on the ledge. One of the Paiutes drew down on him.
I snapped off a shot, splattering the granite by the
Pauite, causing his slug to go wide. On the ledge,
Black Wolf dove for cover.

From where I watched, I saw that the ledge from
which Keen Sighted and his men fired butted against
a shoulder of granite, ending in a sheer drop of over
a hundred feet. Once the fleeing party passed beyond
the shoulder, they would be out of sight.

I snaked my way down through the boulders litter-
ing the slope, trying to remain hidden. The trail they
followed cut down the ridge. I angled down the slope,
hoping to intercept them at the bottom.

I slid to a halt as a slug slammed off a boulder just
in front of me. I jerked around and threw my rifle to
my shoulder. All I saw was the silhouette of a man on
the ridge. I fired just as a powerful blow clubbed me
in the side. The figure's arms flung out, and he fell
backward out of sight.

Doubling over in agony, I squinted against the pain
shooting up my side. A wave of darkness wavered
before me, but I bit my lips until the pain washed away
the darkness. A rush of fear pushed aside the pain
momentarily when I failed to see Susan or her captors.
I blinked my eyes. The trail was empty. They had
disappeared.

Chapter Sixteen

P_{ain} crashed over me. I tensed my muscles and, crouching behind a large boulder, pulled up my shirt. The wound was ugly, but it bled freely. Blood ran down my back. I felt another ragged hole. The slug had passed through, hopefully hitting nothing critical.

I looked around for spiderwebs, but seeing none, tore a strip from my shirt to poke into the wound for a temporary bandage. Clenching my teeth against the pain, I stumbled forward, sweat pouring down my face, my eyes focused on the point where the trail reached the base of the ridge.

Their tracks led deeper into the mountain. I paused to reload the Winchester. I switched it to my left hand and palmed my .45, a more convenient weapon for close work. The trail ascended sharply and veered to the left.

The rocky slopes abounded with sites ideal for ambush. I moved warily. Ahead, metal clattered against rock. I hurried forward. The sun had risen over the crest of the ridges, baking the sandy trail at their base. The pain in my side came now in throbbing waves, dulling my senses.

Once, I stumbled and slammed into a boulder. The searing pain cleared the cobwebs from my head, but now my stomach churned with nausea. I drew a deep breath and continued up the trail. The sheer gray wall of a towering escarpment loomed ahead.

I slowed my pace. Unless the trail took an unexpected turn, the two renegades were at a dead end. I eased forward, my sweaty hand clutching the grip of the cocked .45.

Boulders the size of barns lined the trail. I hesitated at each one, leery of ambush. I realized such caution was slowing me, but I figured I was better off late than dead.

I rounded a bend and jerked to a halt. Ahead was a fissure in the escarpment. The tracks led straight to the opening. I hurried forward, ignoring the last few boulders before the cave.

Just before I reached the mouth of the cave, a click broke the silence. I whirled and threw myself aside, pumping three fast shots in the direction of the faint sound. A Paiute screamed and spun backward.

I took a deep breath and released it slowly. "That just about uses up all my luck," I muttered, knowing full well that there was still one more Paiute out there.

The adrenaline pumping through my body slowed, and the pain returned. Sweat popped out on my forehead. I ejected the spent hulls and inserted three fresh two-hundred-grain slugs in the cylinder.

Taking a deep breath, I entered the cave. Around the first bend, I saw a small opening at the end of the tunnel. As I eased deeper into the cave, the opening grew larger. The cool air dried the perspiration soaking my clothes. Within minutes, a chill swept over me, but I continued moving toward the opening, keeping my ears tuned for any unusual sounds.

A few minutes later, I reached the opening. I hesitated, pausing well back in the cave to see what lay ahead of me. From where I stood, the cave appeared to open into a valley about a mile in width, surrounded at least on two sides by sheer walls of granite reaching high into the sky. As I drew closer to the mouth of the cave, I saw that the third side of the valley was similarly enclosed.

My pulse raced. They were trapped. I grinned despite the throbbing pain.

I peered across the valley. My breath caught when I saw the Comanchero and Sheriff Black dragging Susan down a slope of talus three hundred yards distant. I resisted the urge to race after them.

I scanned the valley. Where was the other Paiute? Behind me? Had he hidden in an offshoot tunnel until I passed? I had no way of knowing.

With Apache fatalism, I raised the Winchester and took aim at the Comanchero. As the muzzle stuck out of the cave, a hand seized it and jerked it from my grasp. My hand flashed for my Colt, but faster than a striking rattler, the Paiute leaped on me from where he had been hiding beside the mouth of the cave, just waiting for me to step outside.

I threw up an arm as he slashed down with his knife. The sharp edge cut deeply into my shoulder, but not so deep as to sever any tendons. Using my right foot, I slammed his left leg from under him.

He grabbed at me as he fell, but I brought my left knee up and caught him under the chin, slamming his head back. The knife clattered from his limp fingers as he hit the ground and rolled down the slope.

I turned to search for the Colt, but in the next instant, I heard the Paiute's footsteps behind me. He leaped as I turned, and the two of us slammed up against the granite. Stars exploded in my head, but I dug the fingers of my hand into his face, trying to shove him back so I could swing a fist.

To the Indian, fists are awkward weapons. He dropped to his knees and grabbed a large rock. As he raised it above his head with both hands, I slammed a gnarled fist into his nose. I felt it break.

He staggered back and shook his head, but I was on top of him in a flash. I caught him in the side with a sharp left hook. When he dropped his hands to cover his stomach, I chopped him down with a right cross that snapped his head around and followed with a left uppercut that caught him on the point of the chin. He slumped to the ground.

I staggered backward, gasping for breath. I sagged against the granite walls.

The renegades were almost a half a mile away, still dragging Susan who by now had spotted me and, with renewed vigor, struggled to escape. Retrieving my Winchester and Colt, I stumbled after them.

When the two men reached the middle of the valley, they paused and looked around. They were too distant to make out the expression on their faces, but by the way they kept looking at each other and then back at me and checking their rifles, I knew they had begun to suspect there was only one exit. And I stood in their path.

Abruptly the Comanchero turned and faced me, forcing Susan to stand in front of him. He threw his rifle aside, pulled his revolver, and held it to her head. She was a small woman, and in her riding clothes, she looked even smaller. He gave her a shove, and she stumbled forward. "*Gringo,*" he called as they drew close. "You hear me?"

The sheriff hurried after the Comanchero, gesturing wildly in my direction.

I levered a shell into the Winchester. "I hear." I winced from the pain in my side, but I managed to line the sights in the middle of his forehead.

He motioned to the cave with the muzzle of his revolver. "You want the woman. I want out. I turn her loose when I reach the cave." He continued toward me as he spoke. "You can have the sheriff here. He is a whining old woman."

"You don't hold those kind of cards, *amigo*. Neither of you. Best you can do is turn her loose and give yourself up to me. I'll do my best to keep the Apache from chopping you both into small pieces and feeding you to the dogs." His face grew larger in my sights. He was fifty feet away now. I took up the slack in the trigger. My finger shook as spasms of pain wracked my body.

Sheriff Black blubbered and threw down his revolver. "I quit, Moore. Don't shoot." His protruding belly shook, and tobacco juice soaked the beard on his chin. "I'll tell you everything."

The Comanchero hissed at him. "Pig! Say nothing."

"No. He can save us. Don't you understand?" whined the sheriff. "Them Apaches'll slice us to pieces." He called out in a loud voice. "You was set up for that treason business, Moore. Simpson had me do it. Me and this greaser here have been payin' Simpson to let prospectors on Apache land. You comin' in woulda ruined a sweet deal for us."

The Comanchero cursed. Before I could move, he turned the revolver on the sheriff and blew the back of his head off. In the next instant, he had the muzzle pressed against Susan's temple.

His face darkened. The revolver shook. "I do not lie, *Gringo*. I have nothing to lose by killing the woman." He came closer. Thirty feet. I could have killed him then without any danger to Susan, but I didn't want to. There had been too much killing. Besides, if I shot him, his reflex action could squeeze the trigger.

Susan's eyes were wide with fear. She looked at me pleadingly.

I tightened my finger on the trigger as I spoke, my voice as firm and level as I could manage. "You've got one last chance. Turn her loose, and I won't kill you." Sweat rolled down my forehead, stinging my eyes. I prayed he would lower his gun.

A sneer curled his lips. A wild look glittered in his eyes. "You talk big, *Gringo*. I show you what big is. I—"

As soon as I saw his trigger finger whiten, I fired. The impact of the slug knocked him backward as if he had been hit between the eyes with a sixteen-pound sledgehammer.

Susan stood frozen, staring at me in disbelief.

Slowly she looked around. She saw the Comanchero sprawled in the grass and turned back to me. Her hands went to her mouth, and she fainted.

I hurried to her. Out of the corner of my eye, I saw the Paiute climb to his feet and disappear into the cave. Slowly Susan came around.

Minutes later, Little Dog and Keen Sighted, with Young Eagle at his heels, found us. "Young Eagle saw you from the ridge. After the Paiute dogs fled, we found your tracks. Even an *ish-kay-nay* like Young Eagle could have followed them in the dark of the moon." Keen Sighted looked at me, his eyes chiding me for my carelessness in leaving such clear sign.

I shrugged and glanced at Young Eagle, who wore a broad grin. I winked at him and turned back to Keen Sighted. "I wanted to make sure you blind old men didn't miss it," I said.

We both grinned and looked at Susan. She forced a wan smile. And at that moment, I knew I wanted nothing more than to have her with me for the rest of my life, of our lives.

A feeling of warmth came over me. For the first time in eleven years, the three of us were together again. No. I glanced at Young Eagle. Make that the "four" of us. I looked at three of them, wishing the moment would never end. I thought of our ranch. And once again the dream returned. My brother and me, and Young Eagle and Susan, who had always been like a sister, but now . . . A strange emotion held me in its grasp, one with which I was not familiar. But it was a pleasant feeling.

However, I didn't have time to enjoy it. From the mouth of the cave, an Apache signaled Keen Sighted. He grunted. "We must go. The bluecoats come."

We hurried from the hidden valley. Now that Susan was safe, I relaxed, but the pain from the wound in my side and shoulder nagged at me. By the time I climbed the ridge to the ledge and wound my way back through the tunnel to the cave entrance, I was staggering on my feet. The last ten minutes, Susan and Young Eagle half-carried me. I shivered with chills.

I slumped to the cave floor beside the fire, relishing its warmth as it flooded over my chilled body. While Keen Sighted and his men went into the next chamber of the cave to ready the ponies, Little Dog and Susan tended my wounds. Behind them, Black Wolf looked on.

From a pouch dangling from his gun belt, Little Dog poured a yellow and white powder into the wounds, monkey flower and clematis. From previous experience, I knew the pain would cease within a few minutes.

"How do you feel?"

I looked up at Susan, who knelt by me with a cup of water in her hand. Tears rimming her eyes sparkled in the firelight. "Believe it or not, I'll live." I squeezed her hand. "How are you?"

She studied me a moment, immediately understanding the implication of my question. "Scared." A pert little grin played over her lips. "Otherwise, I'm fine." She squeezed my hand in return.

I tried to sit up. Susan held me down with a slender hand on my chest. "You need rest."

"No time," I said. "I've got to get Keen Sighted. . . ."

"To do what?" she snapped, cutting me off. "If you're still planning on taking him back for trial, Ben Moore, I'll never speak to you again."

Before I could reply, Young Eagle rushed in. "The bluecoats! They are outside."

Chapter Seventeen

I struggled to my feet as Keen Sighted and his braves hurried back in, leading the ponies.

"What is it you say?" he demanded of Young Eagle.

Young Eagle nodded emphatically. "The bluecoats. They wait for us down below."

A voice sounded from outside. The squeaky voice was unmistakable, Captain R. Albert Simpson. "You inside. Throw your weapons out. You cannot escape."

From the darkness of the cave, we surveyed the troops. I had proof enough to take care of Simpson, but for the present, he was still in charge, and I couldn't risk Keen Sighted and his men's lives. Simpson would shoot them down on sight. But, if I went out under a white flag . . .

Simpson's high-pitched voice echoed across the mountain slope. "Did you hear me? You can't escape.

Put down your weapons and come out with your hands raised.''

I studied his troops again. For once, Simpson was right. I counted our numbers. We were six now, not counting Susan, too few to break through the force facing us. But there was always the rear. The only problem was that we couldn't take the ponies through the narrow passages, and without the ponies in the middle of the desert, we didn't stand a chance against the cavalry. I had to go out myself.

Susan looked up at me. ''Well?''

I frowned at her, not understanding the implication in her question.

She nodded to the bluecoats. ''Here's your chance.''

I stared at her, hurt and disappointed that she really thought I would turn my brother over to the bluecoats. Maybe if the man standing out there had been John Salmon Cook, I would have considered it because Keen Sighted would have been provided every ounce of legal counsel essential for a fair trial, but Albert Simpson was no John Cook. ''Think what you want,'' I said, my tone weary and disheartened.

I glanced at Keen Sighted. He was studying the force before him. Young Eagle stood by his side, glancing up at his hero from time to time, his young eyes filled with admiration.

We were too few to match their strength. Remembering Chato's counsel, I knew that now was the time for wisdom. If we wanted to survive, it had to be by use of our heads, not our strength.

I spoke hurriedly. ''Did they see you?''

Keen Sighted and Young Eagle turned to me.

Young Eagle shook his head. ''No. I was inside when they rode up.''

''Good,'' I replied. ''That means they don't know if we're in here or not.'' I took the reins from Young Eagle and climbed gingerly into the saddle. For a fleeting second, I thought of John Salmon Cook. I had truly planned on taking Keen Sighted in, but now . . . I knew that wherever he was, John Cook would approve of what my plan.

''What do you do?'' Keen Sighted protested.

''Listen to what I say,'' I said in a harsh whisper. ''I know the man out there. He'll be satisfied with me. While I stall them, you slip out the back. They don't know you're in here. When you reach the ridges, you'll be safe. I can handle Simpson in court.''

Susan rushed forward, suddenly understanding my motives. ''Ben, you can't.''

''There's no choice.'' I looked down at Keen Sighted.

Black Wolf spoke up. ''You saved my life. I will go in your place.''

I shook my head. ''It is my job. I must go. I am white, and this calls for the lies only a white man can tell.'' I looked back at Keen Sighted. ''In the Wyoming Tetons is a valley between four peaks. In the middle of the valley is a lake shaped like a horseshoe. It is ours. Take the *ish-kay-nay* and go. When I finish here, I will come.''

Keen Sighted's face darkened. ''No. They will kill you. The captain has given orders to shoot you on sight.''

''Simpson wouldn't take a chance on missing the fun of my trial. But the joke's on him. I have friends too, and when Susan and I tell them of the sheriff's confession, then—''

"You will never be given the chance to speak," said Keen Sighted. "The bluecoats destroy all who support the Apache. I cannot let you do this, my brother."

For several long moments, we looked into each other's eyes. "The bluecoats will have one of us. I know them. My chances are better than yours. You take the boy and your men to Wyoming. Susan and I will be there when we can. I must have Susan here for the trail. She heard the sheriff's admission of the conspiracy with the gold."

Keen Sighted frowned. "I do not know what the sheriff has said, but the bluecoat captain will lie. You will be shot."

"You remember, I'm hard to kill," I said. I grinned and wheeled the bay around.

A shout erupted behind me and a sharp blow exploded a thousand stars in my head. I felt myself falling. I remembered hands grabbing for me, and then nothing.

The sound of retreating hoofbeats cut through the abyss of darkness surrounding me. I forced my eyes open. I lay on the ground, my head in Susan's lap. Warm tears struck my face, tears rolling from her cheeks.

"What . . . what's happening?" My head pounded, and I fought back the threatening darkness.

She looked down, her eyes frantic. "Oh, Ben, stop him, stop him."

I struggled to sit up. "Who? I don't—"

A shout from outside sliced through the murky fog

in my head. Keen Sighted! Instantly, I knew what he had done. I tried to rise, but my muscles refused to respond.

I couldn't see him, but Keen Sighted's clear, deep voice carried through the still air, painting images in my fuzzy brain as he taunted the bluecoats. "The bluecoats are cur dogs, not fit for even the cooking pots of the Paiutes."

From the sound of the hoofbeats, I could tell he was riding back and forth in front of the troops, taunting them.

Simpson called out. "Throw down your weapon and surrender, or we'll fire."

"No," I gasped, rising to my knees and stumbling to the mouth of the cave where the other four Apache watched.

Keen Sighted glanced back at the cave. Our eyes met. With great dignity, he touched his first two fingers to his lips, then extended his forefinger to the sky. Brother.

In the next instant, he spun his pony and laughed at the bluecoats. "Then it is a good day to die," he shouted.

Before I could utter a word, a wild cry burst from Keen Sighted's lips. His pony reared, and he waved his Winchester over his head. Driving his war pony toward the waiting troops, he rose in the stirrups, his long hair flying behind him, his laughter rising above the pounding of the hooves. He jammed the Winchester into his shoulder and began raking the startled troops with his gunfire.

Suddenly, an ear-splitting volley racketed across the slope, and Keen Sighted was flung backward off his pony. His limp body struck the ground and rolled once or twice and then came to a halt.

For a moment, both sides stared numbly at the body of a brave man. Then the silence was shattered by a sob and a scream. I looked around as Young Eagle swung onto his pony.

"No." I stumbled forward, grabbing the youth and yanking him from his pinto.

He turned on me with a savage fury, in my weakened state driving me against the rocky wall. He jerked away and leveled his Winchester on my belly. "Stay away. I must go. The bluecoats . . ."

Stunned by the suddenness of our violence, Little Dog and Black Wolf froze. My eye caught Black Wolf's. The older warrior read the plea in mine. With a quick step forward, he slammed the butt of his rifle into the back of Young Eagle's skull.

I jumped forward, catching the falling youth in my arms and lowering him gently to the ground. Susan cradled the boy's head in her lap.

Outside, Simpson shouted again.

"The *ish-kay-nay*," whispered Black Wolf, looking down at Young Eagle. "He is not hurt?"

I shook my head. "No."

Black Wolf fixed his black eyes on mine. "Take the boy. Leave." He nodded to the rear of the cave. "Our people must not all die here."

Before I could reply, he spun and leaped onto his pony. The remaining two Apache followed his example. Black Wolf looked down at me, a faint smile on his lips. "You and me. I think we could have been friends."

Before I could reply, he yanked his pony around

and slammed his heels into the animal's flanks. With a cry of vengeance, the three Apache raced from the cave, charging the company of waiting bluecoats.

As one, the three warriors jammed their Winchesters into their shoulders and, shouting battle cries, fired as rapidly as they could lever cartridges into the chambers.

Without hesitation, a volley of gunfire raked the three charging Apache. Little Dog alone made it through the first volley, but the second ripped him from his saddle. He hit the ground near Keen Sighted.

With a supreme effort, he squirmed forward, and with his dying breath, touched his fingers to those of Keen Sighted, his chief.

I stared in disbelief at the carnage before me. Susan clutched my arm. I fought the anger coursing through my blood.

There had been enough bloodshed, but I would have my revenge, legally, through the courts. And I would begin with Simpson's deliberate attempt to railroad me to prison with a false charge of treason. The job would be tough, but I was determined to see it through. With Susan to verify Black's confession, I had at least a fifty-fifty chance.

Young Eagle stirred. He opened his eyes. I shook my head. "It is over. You are here, with us. You must live, so our family may continue." I glanced over my shoulder at the troops slowly gathering around my fallen brothers. "Wait in here, Young Eagle. I do not trust the bluecoats. I will send them on their way and come back for you."

He looked up at Susan who confirmed my remarks with a nod.

"I will do as you say," he whispered.

"Good." I looked at Susan. "Let's go."

She helped me from the cave.

Rooney Catlett and Big Bow were the first to reach us. Captain Simpson and Lieutenant Irons were right behind. Simpson smirked. "Now there's treason to add to the charges against you, Moore."

Before I could refute the captain's charge, Catlett spun on the captain, but Lieutenant Irons spoke first. "I believe you're mistaken, Captain. Mr. Rooney here and I both heard you order Mr. Moore to infiltrate the enemy."

Simpson's jaw dropped open. Rooney grinned. "That's right, Captain. And Big Bow, though he be Injun, he heard it too."

Lieutenant Irons added, "So, you see, Captain, counting Mr. Moore here, there's four of us against one of you."

Simpson sputtered. "I'll bring you up on charges for this, Lieutenant. Just you wait and see."

A smile played over Irons's thin lips. "What charges, Captain? You mean about when you and I set Mr. Moore up on that fake treason charge with Sheriff Black in Tucson? Or the times we took a payoff from the sheriff so gold miners could prospect on land that belonged to the Apache?" He shook his head. "I don't think so, Captain. In fact, what I think is that both you and I should tender our resignations to the Army as soon as we get back to camp."

Captain R. Albert Simpson's face grew white as the cottony clouds overhead. Ignoring him, Lieutenant Irons turned to me. His narrow face was pale and drawn, but his eyes gleamed with pride and tears. He swallowed hard. "I don't know about you, Mr. Moore, but right now, I figure my granddaddy is resting a whole lot easier in his grave."

I extended my hand. "I suspect he is, Lieutenant. I suspect he is."

Rooney and Big Bow remained behind to help Susan, Young Eagle, and me bury Keen Sighted and the others. We took them deep into the Baboquivaris where the mountains rose in majestic and forbidding columns, granite sentinels for sleeping giants. There we entombed them, four brave men.

I glanced to the east. Now John Salmon Cook could rest easy. I looked at Young Eagle, his jaw set, his face stoic, but a tear rolled down his cheek.

Taking a deep breath, I paused before I set the last boulder in place. As the rays of the dying sun lit the face of my brother, twenty years of memories filled my head, twenty years of laughter and pain ached in my chest. I shivered and fought back the tears.

Susan's hand touched my arm. "He'll be with the three of us in Wyoming."

Laying my hand on hers, I replied, "I know." I took one last look at the now peaceful face of my brother, *Nay-kay-yen*, and fit the last rock in place.